this side of falling

this side of falling

eunice chan

Published in the United States by Soho Teen
an imprint of Soho Press, Inc.
227 W 17th Street
New York, NY 10011
www.sohopress.com

Copyright © 2025 by Eunice Chan
All rights reserved.

This is a work of fiction. Names, characters, places, and incidents either are the product of the author's imagination or are used fictitiously, and any resemblance to actual persons, living or dead, businesses, companies, events, or locales is entirely coincidental.

Library of Congress Cataloging-in-Publication Data is available upon request.

ISBN 978-1-64129-517-8
eISBN 978-1-64129-518-5

Interior design: Janine Agro, Soho Press, Inc.

Printed in the United States of America

10 9 8 7 6 5 4 3 2 1

EU Responsible Person (for authorities only)
eucomply OÜ
Pärnu mnt 139b-14
11317 Tallinn, Estonia
hello@eucompliancepartner.com
www.eucompliancepartner.com

To my family – for all the light, laughter, and love

Dear Readers, this story contains themes of addiction and suicide, which could be triggers for some audiences. Please read with care.

National Suicide Prevention Hotline: 1-800-273-8255, or call or text 988.

To connect with Suicide Hotlines & Crisis Helplines anywhere in the world, for free, by 24/7 chat, text, and phone: https://findahelpline.com/i/iasp

1

NOT REAL, I tell myself. *Not real.*

My fingers tighten around the handle of my violin case. I see heads turn as I pass the art building and sense the sudden hush. Like this isn't some twisted joke, like Ethan Travvers really—

"Nina!" Someone calls my name.

I glance behind me. Roger Kishimoto is pushing through the crowd, one long, skinny arm waving wildly. He wants me to slow down. Stop.

"Nina Yeung!" he calls again, louder, and even from this distance I can see the worry in his eyes—

No. This isn't *real*. I need to find Beatrice Ryzhenkov. I need to see her. I need to know.

"Nina, wait!" Roger shouts.

But I'm jogging now, my new sneakers slipping on the worn concrete, violin case thumping against my leg. It's the first day back after winter break, the halfway point of my senior year. Lockers slam, voices shout across the outdoor halls.

"You went to Paris for New Year's?"

A short scuffle followed by a burst of laughter. "Hey! That's my new phone!"

"Sorry, I have basketball practice until six. What about tomorrow?"

Bits and pieces of conversations. A collage of lives: past, present, future—

I push past them, turning down one hall then another. *She could be anywhere*, I tell myself. But the familiar bitterness rising in my throat reminds me otherwise.

Just past the history building, I see her: muscular frame, purple hair, tall combat boots.

Before I can cover the ground between us, the warning bell sounds for first period. I'm caught in the sudden exodus from the girls' bathroom. I'm spun around, feet tripping one over the other, falling—

I hit the bank of lockers behind me with a sharp *thunk*. Send the doors rattling against their thin frames. The couple making out just down the row look up, annoyed.

"You okay?"

Someone reaches out to steady me. I don't turn to give an answer because Bea stands just a few feet away at another bank of lockers, her jaw set, fists clenched, knuckles bloody.

"Bea?" I begin, but instead of turning, she slams her fist into Ethan's locker, over and over. Like she's been doing this all morning. Like she's going to do this all day.

"Bea," I say again, needing her to look at me.

But it's as if she doesn't hear me, doesn't see the people who've gathered to stare.

I take a step toward her, my body tense, already bracing for her barbed comment. She never thought I belonged with Ethan.

Slam.

The force of impact makes me flinch.

Slam.

Black mascara runs down Bea's cheeks. I've never seen her cry, didn't think she knew how.

Slam.

Bea's arm drops and she staggers back, gasping for air. In that split second, our eyes meet and I see it. The Truth.

"No—" My voice is lost in the roaring that has started in my ears. Axles jolting, gravel scattering. Steel wheels screaming along steel tracks, picking up speed.

DAVIS HIGH SENIOR ENDS LIFE ON TRACKS. The news app headline on my phone this morning that went on to give a name. Ethan's.

2

BOTH PASSENGER AND freight trains pass through Davis, a university town in northern California located on Interstate 80 between Sacramento and the Bay Area.

The train station downtown, the railroad tracks, the blast of the train horns are all familiar to me, as much a part of life as the surrounding farmland and the fifty-plus miles of trails and bike lanes connecting the community.

But nothing felt familiar as I biked to school this morning. Instead of the rumble of the early morning trains passing through, the only sound I could hear was the heavy thudding of my own heart.

It wasn't him, I told myself as I biked past the gourmet grocery store, the bank, the donut shop. The name in the news release had to be a mistake. After all, there are over five hundred seniors at Davis High—

I skidded to a stop, my way blocked.

ROAD CLOSED. The large rectangular sign was mounted on the traffic barricades at the bottom of the overpass bridging the tracks. The same overpass Ethan and I often crossed on our bikes, fighting our way up the steep incline and coasting down the other side.

Behind me, cars turned, following the smaller black and orange signs marking the detour.

No. I shook my head. *No.* But the thudding in my chest only grew heavier.

Now, as I approach the double doors to first period orchestra, I swallow hard, trying and failing to block out the image of Bea in front of Ethan's locker, mascara tracks running down her cheeks, her knuckles bloody.

Not real, I tell myself.

Those words are a wall, a wedge, between me and the Truth I saw in Bea's eyes.

"You heading in?" the timpani player asks, holding open the door.

Yes. No. I don't know.

Somehow, I force a nod, and, holding tight to the handle of my violin case, I step inside.

Symphony orchestra is always chaos the first day back after winter break. Folding chairs topple. The bassoonists and bass clarinetist brawl, three against one. The flautists shelter behind a bank of music stands a respectable distance away.

At the other end of the orchestra room, the violists cluster in solidarity, whispering furiously. Apparently, their section leader has turned in her viola, picked up the sousaphone, and joined the pep band. Who *does* that?

I head straight for the violin section. But out of the corner of my eye, I see the lights on in the small office by the double doors. Mr. Martinez, our orchestra teacher, works on his laptop, a tin of breath mints and three cups of coffee lined up on his desk. Fuel for the morning ahead.

I draw in a shaky breath—*Not real.*

Davis High is a nationally ranked high school with a reputation for strong academics—and an exceptional music program. Mr. Martinez's standards for performance are high, and getting his letter of recommendation for my college and music-intensive applications last fall meant everything to me.

I know I should go to his office and talk about the string quartet's winter repertoire. Get his thoughts on any new pieces we should consider. After all, Mr. Martinez has given me the lead role for the string quartet this year, a role I've been fumbling.

I desperately need to get back on track and in his good graces. At least that's what I told myself all winter break. But now I can't think, can't speak. In my head I'm replaying that split second when Bea's eyes met mine this morning.

Not real.

"Excuse me . . . Sorry." I jostle down the row of violinists, keeping my gaze averted, sheet music clutched to my chest. I don't want them to talk to me. Don't want them to look at me.

"Hey, Nina! What'd you do over break?"

"I like your jacket."

"Are those new sneakers?"

I do love my new high-top sneakers, the down jacket that makes it look like I actually spend time outside. Likely on a glacier. But I don't smile, don't say a word. Their question marks hang in the air as I take the second chair next to Roger's girlfriend, Lucy Beyers.

Not first, but second chair.

Setting the sheet music on the stand between us, I open my violin case and check the tension of the bow hairs, apply rosin. Try to ground myself in the familiar, the routine. I remind myself that second chair is fine, just fine, even though it's not.

The challenge for Lucy's first chair was held the first week of December. Three of us in the violin section competed for her spot as the concertmistress. There was a blind audition, everyone playing the same passage. Even though my thoughts were tied up with Ethan—the significance of our kiss—I was certain I had it this time, that edge. Enough to oust Lucy, who just transferred to our high school from Boise, Idaho, this school year.

The results were posted the last day before winter break.

I bite my lip, fighting the rising panic spreading across my chest, down my arms, to my fingertips.

Next to me, Lucy crosses and uncrosses her tiny penny-loafered feet. She's wearing another hand-embroidered sweater from her Etsy shop, which features clothing with messages like BE KIND or EMPATHY IS COOL. Today, it's JUST BREATHE.

I shudder.

Twisting a strand of her glossy shoulder-length red hair, Lucy clears her throat with a delicate "A-hem." I pretend not to notice.

See you tomorrow, then?

My text to Ethan at ten last night as I was getting ready for bed.

Yeah.

He'd texted back at ten-forty. Where was he then? At home, getting ready to leave? On his bike? On the overpass?

He was pronounced dead at eleven-fifteen.

My knuckles tighten as if, like Bea, I too need to punch something, anything. I feel the cake of rosin in my palm flex, crack.

"So," Lucy chirps, louder this time, forcing her way back

into my peripheral vision. "How was the Young Musicians Intensive? You just got back, right?"

I know it's not the question she wants to ask. *Are you okay? I am so, so sorry to hear what happened. Let me know if there is anything I can do to help. Anything.*

"Right," I manage, teeth gritted, fingers still gripping the rosin. "It was fine."

Lucy's smile widens. An invitation to elaborate on my week and a half in Colorado eating, sleeping, and breathing with some of the best teen musicians in the United States.

I don't.

"Great!" she exclaims, reaching for her sheet music. "So glad to hear! I mean, the bios for the YMI instructors are *amazing*. I wanted to go just for Andre Valdecci but I had the embroidery conference in Texas and couldn't do both . . ."

The can lights above me are too bright. My fingers tremble as I slip my cracked rosin back into its drawstring bag. I shouldn't have gone to the Intensive over the break. I should have stayed here with Ethan. Maybe if I had, everything would be different.

"Seats!" Mr. Martinez takes the stand and motions for Lucy.

My stomach sinks as Lucy walks primly to the front of the room. Lifting her violin, she plays the perfect A.

Section by section we tune to her instrument. Hers, not mine. Woodwinds first, then brass, then lower strings, then violins. The sounds dissonant at first, then melding together into one.

I pretend to study the sheet music as Lucy returns to her seat beside me. But the pages are just a jumble of meaningless lines and dots instead of notes and staff, rhythm and sound.

Mr. Martinez directs us to the third movement of Tchaikovsky's *1812 Overture*. As if on autopilot, my fingers move along the fingerboard of my violin, my bow pulling and tugging against the strings. Every movement practiced, mechanical—empty.

The notes rise higher, faster. The music swelling, wailing, crashing against me.

I wait. For that moment when the tangle of my thoughts unravels. When the music takes over and I'm lost in its sweetness and power. But all I feel is pain.

3

I DON'T LIKE pain in any form. Whether it's needles, the dentist, or working out.

Maybe that's why I chose to focus on the violin instead of playing volleyball like my older sister, Carmen. I've seen her suffer. All that running and weight training, the inevitable injuries, and the physical therapy and acupuncture appointments that follow.

But the pain gripping me now is different than Carmen's. It's in my head. It's in my chest. A slow tearing, like fingers wrenching me apart from the inside. It *hurts*.

As soon as first period ends, I'm out of my seat. I've already got a plan worked out to get back to the bridge. It will make me miss at least the first part of second period physics—and tarnish my otherwise perfect attendance.

But I need to see. I need to know.

Locking up my violin, I speed walk toward the double doors of the orchestra room. But Peter Kapoor with his tiny body and giant cello case block my way.

"Hey, Nina," Peter says in his high-pitched, whiny voice. "Is quartet practice at your house Friday?"

Is it? I'm not sure of anything right now except I need to go, get out of here.

"Seven, right?" the violist for the string quartet, Madison

Clark, asks as she shambles up behind me in pajama pants and an oversized hoodie.

"Nina." Mr. Martinez motions me to come up to the front of the room. "Do you have a minute?"

The room seems to spin. I barrel past Peter, catching a glimpse of the perplexed look on Mr. Martinez's face as the double doors close behind me. Outside the orchestra room, my legs feel unsteady, like I'm walking across the deck of a pitching ship. The crowds in the hallways jostle me. I duck my head, keeping my eyes averted as I make my way across the open campus to the bike cage.

"Did you know they closed the bridge in *both* directions this morning?" A tall girl with lash extensions passes me, her car keys jangling in her hand.

"Why?" her friend asks. "I thought the tracks ran *under* the bridge."

"Exactly," the tall girls says. "I had to take this big, long detour—"

My chest squeezes. I gasp, my palm pressing instinctively against it. Like I can stop the hurt this way.

People stream past the bike cage in pairs, in groups, heading to their next class. The way I should be heading to my next class so I don't get marked tardy, or worse, absent.

Instead, I walk through the chain-link gate and fight my way down the rows of bikes until I get to mine. My fingers shake as they fumble with the combination lock.

It wasn't him, I tell myself, *there's been some mistake*. But the words aren't shielding me like I need them to.

I roll my bike out of the cage and swing my leg over the frame, my right foot finding the toe clip, my thumb and fingers wrapping loosely around the handlebars. Faces and voices blur as I pick up speed. In the distance, I hear the warning bell sound for second period.

I pedal harder, my jaw clenched and knuckles white, following the route I had mentally mapped during orchestra. I cut through the backside of the park, biking fast under the bare branches of large trees, avoiding the puddles of water from the rain last night. I'm flying by the time I pass the wooden play structure, then the arts center.

A train whistle blares, breaking the silence that haunted me on the ride to school this morning.

The traffic barricades are still up on this side of the bridge. I bank hard to slow down and weave between them, catching the back of my hand on a sharp corner. It leaves a scrape, but I don't even feel the sting.

Shifting gears, I ride uphill. My breath comes in short, hot gasps. Every push of the pedals brings me closer. I hear it. I see it. Steel wheels jolting along steel tracks. Gravel scattering, the ground trembling.

Ten yards, five yards, two. I ditch the bike.

The whistle splits the air. Even up on the bridge, I feel the weight of the approaching train pressing against my chest, feel the rocking rhythm of its axles in my jaw. Tears well in my eyes and a scream catches in my throat. A physics equation comes to me.

Momentum is mass times velocity. Mass times . . .

Gripping the wire mesh of the safety fence, I stare down at the train as it passes, watching until the last carriage disappears underneath the bridge.

"Miss, I'm going to need you to step back."

Eleven hours. It's been eleven hours since Ethan climbed

the safety fence on the overpass. Jumped onto the tracks in front of an approaching freight train.

"Miss—"

Why? Why did he do it?

I swallow hard, staring down at the now empty tracks. The steel rails stand out like bright lines against the dark wood ties. Along the edges of the tracks, pools of standing rainwater reflect the pale, cloudless sky. The sound of birds calling in the brown grove of trees shriek in the sudden silence.

The news crew is long gone and the scene below sterilized, as if nothing ever happened here.

"—this area is still off limits." The heavy tread of boots grind to a halt behind me.

I turn slowly, my fingers pressed to my lips.

The policeman holds a bike that's been tagged and labeled. An older-style road bike with a tube frame and brown handlebar tape. Ethan's.

A wail begins from somewhere deep inside. My legs finally buckle and the ground rushes upward.

What are you thinking, Nina? You know better than to make a scene. I hear Mom's voice in my head, chastising me.

But it's too late. Jerking sobs wrack my chest. My fingers grip the crumbled pavement. I taste the tears and snot slick-. ening my face.

A burst of static. Garbled words on the radio, a curt response.

Still the sounds come out of me, guttural and inhuman.

More footsteps. Radios. Voices.

I can't move, I can't breathe.

He's not coming back.

4

HOW CAN SOMEONE just disappear? Like a silk handkerchief vanishing under a magician's sleight of hand. No warning, no explanation. Here one moment, gone the next.

It shouldn't be that simple.

I want to rewind the clock to the very beginning. Back to a time when there weren't questions or friction, only possibilities. To that day in October, three months ago, when I first met Ethan.

It was first period orchestra. Mr. Martinez had arranged for Lucy and me to meet with the school's resident artist to discuss the design for this year's orchestra shirts instead of attending class.

I'd heard the name Ethan Travvers. I knew he was the guy who designed school posters and painted some of the murals around campus.

In tenth grade, while the rest of us struggled to transition from junior high to high school, he seemed to find his footing quickly, rising up the social ladder. Rumors spread, even to me, that upperclassmen were inviting him to parties.

Then, in junior year, he suddenly dropped out. Some said he went to Da Vinci, the charter academy in town. Others said he switched over to independent study. At least one person claimed he was in the UK, shadowing street artists. It seemed no one really knew his whereabouts. But in a school of eighteen hundred students, he'd only been a name to me. Our paths had never crossed.

He was back now, at the start of senior year. His return so quiet, I'd heard nothing of it until Mr. Martinez sent out the calendar invite for the orchestra shirt design.

"You think that's him?" Lucy asked as we approached the school library, a white stucco building with a vaulted roof.

The guy standing at the library entrance was medium height with a slim build and light brown hair. I found my gaze lingering on his fitted gray T-shirt and the cut of his dark-wash jeans—not too tight, not too loose—before finally shifting my eyes to the heavy-duty canvas messenger bag slung across his chest.

Lucy had spent the walk over here sharing unsolicited tidbits she'd heard about Ethan. It seemed he kept mostly to himself now and to the goth/stoner set.

"Maybe . . . ?" I offered, surprised that he didn't have the dark, brooding look of the creative-types I'd pictured in my head. Maybe he wore the artist's angst as a facial expression. Not that I could confirm this since his head was turned, as if he was expecting us to approach from the other side of campus.

"Hi! You must be Ethan," Lucy said, walking straight up to him, her hand extended.

I admired her bold approach.

"That's me." Ethan stared at Lucy's outstretched hand like he wasn't quite sure what to do with it. "And you're—?"

"Lucy," she answered, her smile brighter than normal. "And this is Nina."

Ethan turned to me and I felt a strange jolt, like I'd pricked my finger or stepped on hot pavement in bare feet. I hadn't expected . . . *this*. Tanned skin, high cheekbones, light brown, almost blond, hair falling forward to frame green-gold eyes.

"Hey," I somehow managed to mumble, then immediately looked away. He'd just taken me by surprise. That was it, end of story.

"You designed this year's homecoming shirts, right? They were *amazing*," Lucy gushed as the three of us headed into the library. She was a little too enthusiastic about things, in my opinion. "I bought one in the gray and one in the royal blue."

"Glad they worked out," Ethan said lightly.

"Absolutely." Lucy smiled. "Unfortunately, I can't say the same for our orchestra shirts. They've always been a bit of a flop. Not for any lack of effort. Several of us submitted designs and we voted. It's just . . ."

"Not your thing?" he said.

"Maybe," Lucy admitted, her tone reluctant.

I tried not to roll my eyes. *You can't be great at everything.*

"Well—" Ethan flipped to a fresh page in his sketchpad and I thought I saw a flash of resignation in his face. Like he was forced to do this, forced to be here. "Where do you want to start?"

Lucy cleared her throat daintily. She'd been doing that ever since her bout of pneumonia the month before. "For theme, we're thinking: freedom."

"We are?" I turned, surprised.

"Yes. Unless . . ." Lucy's brow furrowed. "You had something different in mind?"

"I didn't know we had decided on anything." I shrugged. "That's all."

"Well." Lucy sat up straighter. "I'm just throwing ideas out there."

"*Your* ideas—"

"Freedom," Ethan said quickly, jotting it down. "Okay."

"And for the shirt color we're thinking black," Lucy added, ignoring me. "With DAVIS HIGH SCHOOL ORCHESTRA in light blue lettering framed by white baby wings."

"'White baby wings?'" Ethan repeated, and this time it was his brow that furrowed.

"*And* flying music notes." Lucy fluttered her fingertips.

Ethan hesitated, his gaze sliding toward me.

I shook my head. *Not a chance.*

"The music notes float on the breeze created by the baby wings," Lucy expounded, as if that would make the concept less nauseating. "You know, the idea that music sets you free."

Ethan stared.

"Maybe," I interjected, tapping the top of his sketch pad, "we could also work in a bald eagle soaring into a sunset."

"We're having a serious conversation here, Nina," Lucy snapped.

"I am serious."

"Eagles *do* symbolize freedom," Ethan offered in a helpful tone. "As well as courage, strength, resilience . . ."

"Not a good idea," Lucy said, narrowing her blue eyes at me.

Why, exactly, was I here again? Oh, right. Someone had to be the voice of reason.

"Fine." I shrugged. "Why don't we ask Ethan for his ideas? He's the expert."

I glanced over just in time to see Ethan's brows raise at the word "expert."

"How about this," he said, sketching in quick bold strokes. "We use the black shirt, but have the fingerboard of a cello running vertically down the front. White lines against the black, very stylistic. DHS ORCHESTRA in old stone lettering, narrow, across the chest." He flipped the sketchpad around.

I considered myself a connoisseur of the performing arts rather than the fine arts, but nevertheless I felt drawn to the bold, clean lines, the simplicity.

"Obviously it will look better once I get it on my tablet," he explained, a faint flush creeping up his neck as he glanced down and away. "Have a chance to play around with shading and font."

"Oh no," Lucy effused. "This is incredible. *Exactly* what I had in mind," she said, even though it was nothing like what she had in mind. "If we could just add the white baby wings on either side of the—"

"No," I deadpanned.

"—fingerboard. What do you think?" Lucy pressed, ignoring me again.

But Ethan was looking my way, his hazel eyes more green than gold, something like a smile playing across his perfect lips.

I glanced down at the table, fighting the sudden tightness in my throat, the pressure in my chest. I tried to take a breath, shake it off, but I couldn't.

Because Ethan Travvers was gorgeous.

5

YEUNGS DON'T MAKE a scene.

It's one of Mom's Basic Rules—or MBRs, as Carmen called them. Growing up, there was zero tolerance for meltdowns in the toy aisle or in a restaurant, for public arguments, or for anything that could draw negative attention from anyone, in public, ever.

There are other MBRs that Mom made a point of drilling into me and my sister since we were kids. Rules like *Yeungs always look presentable*, which entails never leaving the house in loungewear or with bed head, and *Yeungs are never late*, which means we're expected to be five minutes early to everything.

The repercussions for breaking an MBR have been swift and memorable. Getting enrolled in Kumon for extra math tutoring whether you needed it or not, picking the aphids off Mom's garden roses with a pair of tweezers and a paper cup, mandatory weekly phone calls with Grandma in Mandarin only.

Riding home in Mom's white BMW SUV, her pristine leather back seats folded down to carry my less-than-pristine bike, I wince as I think of the MBR I broke—*Yeungs don't make a scene*.

Mom is dressed in a sharp navy pantsuit and heels, her

above-the-shoulder black hair sleek and styled. She's a section manager now, having taken two promotions in the four years since Dad secured his third pharmaceutical patent and found a business partner, Rich Bashir, to help him "grow the startup." She must have been in the middle of her morning staff meeting when she got the call from the police to pick me up.

My chest shudders with the last of my sobs as I dab my swollen eyes with a crumpled tissue. Second period physics, which is where I'm supposed to be right now, feels distant and hazy, like it's part of someone else's life.

"So, what's this about?" Mom finally asks, breaking the silence. She keeps her gaze fixed out the windshield at the four cyclists in the turn lane in front of us. "It's that boy, isn't it?" Her tone is hard and accusing.

Ethan, I want to correct. She saw the news release this morning too. *He has a name and you know it.*

But she's never acknowledged him, never asked for an introduction. To her, Ethan was simply a distraction, one I should have quickly and neatly eliminated. After all, *Yeungs don't date until senior year of college.*

I never had a problem with this MBR like Carmen did. She was always in a relationship or just getting out of one. I never understood the draw. I didn't get how it could possibly be worth the constant tension, the battles with Mom, the curfews and restrictions that followed.

And then, last October, I met Ethan.

"He was never a good influence on you," Mom continues when I don't respond. "Always pulling you away from your schoolwork, your college applications, your SAT prep, for what? T-shirt designs? Paintings on walls?"

He's dead! I want to shout. Instead, I close my eyes and turn away from her.

Mom isn't one for grieving. She's the oldest of four, and Grandma told me that when Grandpa died, Mom never shed a tear. Instead, she just worked harder in her college studies, eventually graduating summa cum laude, setting a good example for her three younger brothers. It was what was expected.

If only we could all be so resolved.

Mom's still talking, laying out the terms of my new restrictions as we roll slowly past the large custom homes on our street and pull into our driveway.

The crew of landscapers tending the elaborate xeriscape in our front yard looks up as I bolt from Mom's car before she even gets it in park.

"Nina!" Mom calls after me. I look back briefly to see her nod at the landscapers, trying to moderate the irritation in her tone. "We still need to unload your bike!"

But I'm already opening the front door, letting myself in. Leaving my high-top sneakers in the large white-tiled foyer, I pound up the stairs to my room and slam the door hard. The frame with my first-place certificate from last year's Mozart competition clatters to the ground.

He's not coming back.

I fall onto my bed with a strangled scream as the wrenching pain in my head and chest grip me again.

I was supposed to see him today in the graphic arts room at lunch. We'd been messaging back and forth the last ten days while I was at YMI. Rebuilding, I thought, the rapport we had before Bea stepped in and ruined everything.

And now he's gone.

My phone buzzes in my backpack, a new message brightening the screen of my watch. It's my physics lab partner asking why I'm not in class.

I groan, rolling over on my bed and pulling my knees up to my chest.

Below me, I hear the garage door rumble closed and Mom drive away. I exhale, but there's no relief. Outside, the buzz and whine of the weed whackers seem to go on forever. Like the soundtrack to Mom's need for perfection in all things: work, house, yard, family. Everything needs to look just right.

Are you here?

A familiar twinge of guilt pricks me as I glance down an hour later to see another new message on my watch, this one from Roger. He's Mom's best friend's son and our old neighbor, my friend for as far back as I can remember. He had tried to flag me down this morning and I just . . . ignored him. He should be used to it by now. I've ignored him ever since I met Ethan.

Where? I force myself to type back, trying to ease that guilt with a reply.

The gym. Mandatory assembly.

I draw in a sharp breath, my throat tightening.

Where are you sitting? Roger asks.

A school-wide assembly. The implementation of postvention protocols. The offering of counseling services. A chance to sit together with others in the After.

But instead, I'm here in my room, alone.

Alone.

A chill crawls up my spine as I start to type back. It's what I wanted, right? To be left alone with my thoughts, my pain?

The four white walls of my room start to blur as wrenching fingers slowly tear my heart.

In my head, I replay the last messages in my text string with Ethan, hearing our voices as if in dialogue.

See you tomorrow, then?

Yeah.

There were supposed to be so many more moments for us.

I need you, I whisper silently, fervently. *Don't you know that?*

For a second, I can picture him here in this room. I can almost sense the solidness of his presence, catch the light, clean scent of his cologne. Two hot tears squeeze from my eyes and slide down my cheeks.

Stay with me, I plead.

But my head spins and his image fades and I fall into a dreamless sleep.

6

A CAR HORN beeps in the driveway.

Stifling a groan, I sit up, pressing a hand to my face. My throat is sore, my muscles ache, and my eyes are two swollen pillowy lumps. Instead of my pink and white pajamas, I'm wearing the same jeans and light gray sweater I wore—

Yesterday.

It all rushes back to me: Bea at the lockers, the bike ride to the bridge, the car ride home. Did I really sleep for nineteen hours? Who put my covers over me?

"Nina!" Mom raps sharply on my bedroom door, a noisy staccato. "Roger's here. Don't let him wait."

Roger. I feel a pang of guilt as I remember the way I left him hanging yesterday. First in the school halls and then in our text messages. But I don't know why he's here, now, waiting. Unless Mom arranged for him to—

"You're not even up!" Mom exclaims, letting herself into my room when I don't respond. "Do you know what time it is?"

Striding across my room, she yanks the covers back, leaving me no choice but to stumble out of bed. I should have known that staying home from school yesterday was a one-time exception. "You need to hurry, Nina!" she admonishes.

"I don't need a ride," I grumble, shivering in the cold.

Mom never turns up the heat as much as I'd like her to. She claims it's for energy conservation, but I think it's just her selective frugality.

"Yes," Mom says, firmly. "You do." She straightens the comforter on my bed and plumps the pillows, her movements practiced and precise. "Roger will pick you up and drop you off for as long as your dad and I see fit."

"*What?*" My fingers curl into fists. I know I broke an MBR, but isn't there consideration for shock, for loss? More than anything, I want her to ask how I'm holding up. Maybe even say she's sorry about what happened, acknowledge Ethan by name.

Her gaze slides down to my clenched fists and for a second, I see something in her face shift, soften. But when I blink, it's gone.

"Make sure to comb your hair," Mom snaps. "It looks like a bird's nest."

Right. Because that's what matters right now, my *hair*.

Roger's ancient Geo Metro is idling in the driveway when I finally walk out of the house. Despite the low morning temperatures, the manual windows of his car are cranked all the way down. Roger's long, skinny arm dangles out the driver's side window, his fingers drumming a bouncy rhythm on the dented door.

Before getting a full view, I already know he's wearing a Kirkland Signature shirt with the Kirkland Signature cargo shorts he wears all year round. Nobody loves Costco more than Roger's family.

"Nina Y," he calls as I approach, but his voice lacks its usual exuberance and his dark brown eyes are pained, worried.

Forcing a nod, I duck quickly into the front passenger

seat. Pray he doesn't notice that my eyes are swollen, my face a mess. I try to remember the last time we've been alone, anywhere, but my mind draws a blank.

"Of course, you remember Annabel." Roger backs slowly down the driveway and into the empty street. His tone is friendly, conversational.

He's still the same nice-to-a-fault guy that Carmen and I grew up with. The one who invited us to youth group events at the local church four years ago when things at our home were tense and heavy, my parents consumed with the launch of Dad's startup.

"Sure." I survey the pitted dash, the plastic-wrapped seats. Hazard a glance at the odometer. If anything, Annabel looks exactly the same, or perhaps worse for wear.

"She's basically brand new. I just changed her oil, flushed her fluids—"

"So . . . is that what's on the driveway?"

Roger jams the brakes, his face paling. "Uh, that was there before."

"You know it wasn't."

"It's got to be condensation. It happens when there's fog. Nothing to worry about."

"What fog?" I shoot him a look. "My mom just had the driveway power washed. If it stains, she's going to freak."

"Er." Roger grimaces, undoubtedly flipping through his memory bank of my mom's best lectures. "I guess I'll have to take my chances then."

"Your funeral," I say, not thinking about my choice of words until an awkward silence falls.

"Um." Roger hesitates, glancing cautiously at me. "About Ethan—"

My throat tightens. "We don't need to talk about it," I say quickly.

"I tried to find you at the assembly yesterday," Roger continues. "Figured you needed some company."

"I went home."

"Right," Roger says. "It's just..." He bites his lip and runs a hand through his coarse, home-cut dark hair. "I'm sorry."

"You don't have to be." I keep my tone clipped, trying to end the conversation before it begins. After all, I should be the one telling Roger I'm sorry. Not just about yesterday, but for cutting him out of my life once I met Ethan.

"I mean, I know you two were together and—"

"Were we?"

The question slips out unintentionally. It hangs in the space between us, this sore I've kept hidden, this equation I could never balance.

"Well, yeah," Roger says, glancing quizzically at me. "You've been inseparable since October..."

I shake my head. Roger plows on, but the words blur in my ears. He could never take a hint.

Of course, he doesn't know that I never knew where I stood with Ethan. That Ethan could be warm and close one moment and cold and distant the next. That I always had to watch what I said and how I said it. So I quickly learned to study his every gesture, his every look, his every word. Adding and subtracting, needing someway, somehow to define the relationship since Ethan never did.

Even though he was the one who started it. Sending me a direct message, inviting me to go downtown with him to check on the screen-printing order for the orchestra shirts. Pulling me out of my regimented world and into his.

7

MY WORLD BEFORE Ethan was structure, rules, ruthless predictability.

I thrived on scheduling every moment of every day. I had goals for my senior year of high school—getting into YMI, leading the string quartet, performing my senior violin recital, and getting into at least one of my top three music colleges. Distractions were out of the question.

But after that day I met Ethan at the library, I found myself looking for him in the halls, during lunch, and as I walked to and from the bike racks. I wanted to see him again, even imagined the kind of conversations we could have. I studied the murals he'd done around school, marveling at the clean lines, the stark contrasts, the layered themes.

Heading across campus, I'd pass the art buildings and wonder if he was there designing something on the computers in the graphic arts room or working on a new sketch in the drawing and painting classroom. But I never caught even a glimpse of him. I told myself it was probably for the best.

It wasn't until later that I discovered our paths hadn't crossed this year for a reason.

His new social circle, the goth/stoner set, did not intersect with mine, the tight-laced/high-achieving/classically-trained contingent. Besides, I was so busy, I hardly engaged in any social activities even within my own circle. I had the lead role for the string quartet to focus on, violin pieces to perfect and record for my YMI and music college applications. There were the essays I needed to write for the University of California schools and select Ivy Leagues Mom expected me to apply to. Not to mention studying for the SATs—my final chance to improve my score was just a month away.

Even though I didn't see Ethan, I did hear from him. As promised, he'd sent Lucy and me a digital copy of the final orchestra shirt design. The email was annoyingly terse, with "see attached" and no signature line.

I told myself I must have imagined it, that connection I felt in the library. It was just a passing moment after all, a blip, when I found him looking my way, his hazel eyes more green than gold, just a hint of a smile playing across those perfect lips.

I tried to shake off my disappointment, but it clung to me.

I was cutting across the quad on my way to pick up a letter of recommendation from Mr. Martinez during lunch when I finally saw Ethan. He was sitting at the far end of one of the picnic tables, his head bent over his sketchpad, earbuds in. The afternoon sun brought out the golden tints in his hair.

I felt my breath catch.

He was wearing the same fitted gray shirt and dark-wash jeans that caught my eye that first day. They still looked good on him. Better.

Keep walking, I told myself. *Don't stare.*

But I found my steps slowing, my gaze drifting to the muscular girl with purple hair standing on top of the table in tall black combat boots. A guy with long locs, a monobrow, and a black cape was tossing grapes to her and she was catching them between her teeth, her torso compressing and extending like the bellows of an accordion.

"That's five!"

"And ... six."

"Seven!"

Shouts and whistles erupted from the table. All eyes were on her. All except Ethan's.

She paused as if sensing this. Her kohl-lined eyes swept down the table to where Ethan sat, doodling, lost in his own thoughts.

A slow grin spread across her face. Silently, she motioned for the bag of grapes.

"Don't do it, Bea!" someone hissed, as she plucked out the biggest one.

But already, she was sighting down the length of her arm, her lips pursed. A quick flick of the wrist and it was a bull's-eye, splattering right between Ethan's brows.

The table exploded with laughter.

"Gotcha!" She snort-laughed, pelting him with more grapes from the bag.

What are you doing? That's disgusting! I wanted to shout at her.

But Ethan just reached up and brushed away the sticky bits, continuing to sketch like this kind of thing happened every day.

I shook my head, forcing myself to keep walking right past his table.

So, this was where he ate lunch, these were his friends. He seemed content in their company. Yet I couldn't shake the feeling that something was off, like a string on my violin that was nearly, but not quite, in tune. How did someone who was at the top of the social ladder sophomore year, end up *here*?

"Hey."

My steps faltered. For a second, I wasn't sure if I had heard right. Did he—?

I hazarded a glance back at the picnic table to find Ethan looking at me, a smile in his hazel eyes.

"Hey," I mumbled, and it was hard to breathe, hard to look straight back at him.

It was just one word, hardly a conversation, but as I turned away, I felt buoyant, euphoric, hopeful. Was this the draw for Carmen? Were these the feelings that made it worth the endless battles with Mom?

The DM from Ethan came later that night, asking if I wanted to bike to the screen-printing shop downtown after school the next day.

I had things already on my schedule, things that were important, things that needed to be done. Besides, Mom expected me to come straight home after school—

Yeah, I replied, typing quickly and hitting send before I could change my mind.

8

THE THING ABOUT Roger is that he doesn't *quit*. Even when I tried to cut him out of my life last fall, he was always still texting, calling, inviting me to events with the youth group.

"Just bring Ethan," he'd say, undeterred by my increasingly vague excuses for not showing up to the scavenger hunt, volunteer event, bowling night, etc.

"There's something wrong with that guy," Ethan had remarked once after Roger had pulled an elaborate U-turn on the road just so he could roll down his window and say hi as Ethan and I biked home from school.

I'd felt a rush of defensiveness at his remark. *You don't know him!* I wanted to tell Ethan. *He's just being nice. It's who he is.*

Even as a kid, Roger was always doing things like holding doors open. Not just for me and Carmen, but for everyone else in the vicinity too. If there was a spill, he was the first one on the scene cleaning it up. When Carmen went through a bossy phase, I bristled at her every request, an adamant no already perched on my lips. But Roger played along—holding her purse, her jacket, her umbrella while she "touched up" her face in the nearest public restroom, or running to the store for her favorite orange juice when she was "parched."

As we hit puberty, Roger shot up in height but stayed skinny. Unreachable object on the top shelf? He was your guy to retrieve it. In fact, he was everyone's top-shelf guy. This made trips to the grocery store rather lengthy.

But now, as I'm riding to school with Roger, I can't help but wish he would quit—quit trying to cheer me up, quit trying to get me to talk, quit being so ... *nice*.

"Okay, Nina," Roger says as we approach the school parking lot. "I know we're running a little late so I'll drop you off at the curb and then find parking."

"It's fine," I say. "Just park."

I'm dreading walking into school looking the way I do—eyes swollen from yesterday's crying jag, my face a mess. Breaking Mom's Basic Rule that *Yeungs always look presentable*.

"Wait . . . what's this?" Roger shouts excitedly. "Someone's backing out! Hold tight!"

I grip both sides of the plastic-wrapped seat as Roger careens into the parking lot and slides into the newly vacated parking spot, barely missing the side mirrors of the cars next to us. It's still mystifying to me how Roger actually passed his driver's test.

"I think it's going to rain," he says, squinting at the sky as he climbs out of his car. "Did you bring an umbrella?"

"No." I swing my backpack over my shoulder. The last thing I thought about checking this morning was the weather.

"Hang on, I've got one you can use," Roger offers, turning to rummage through the clutter in the back seat of his car.

"It's fine," I say and start across the parking lot, heading to first period orchestra.

"Hey, stop walking so fast." Roger jogs up beside me,

holding out an enormous black-and-white Costco umbrella that could easily provide coverage for five people. How that umbrella fits in the back seat of his Geo Metro is yet another mystery. "You need this."

"Roger, seriously."

"Nina, seriously."

"Roger . . . !"

"Nina . . . !"

"I. Don't. Need. The. Umbrella." I say each word slowly, deliberately, maintaining full eye contact, or as full as I can manage with my puffy pillow eyes.

"Okie doke," Roger says and swings the umbrella over his shoulder. "I'll see you at the library after school then?"

"Right," I manage, too worn out to argue. It is The Plan after all, Roger chauffeuring me to and from school for as long as my parents see fit. Repercussions of leaving school, making a public scene.

I keep my head down and my shoulders hunched as I hurry toward the orchestra practice room. Aware that with yesterday's all-school assembly, now *everyone* knows. Even those who hadn't seen the news release. There will only be more questions, more looks—

Out of the corner of my eye, I catch a splash of color. Red. As I turn to look, I notice other colors: yellow, white, pink, blue. It's those fake, plastic and cloth flowers that take up a whole aisle in a home-goods or arts-and-crafts store. They're stacked in front of Ethan's last and largest mural, which features the Blue Devils logo in the foreground and a watermarked background highlighting the sciences, arts, and athletics. Everything painted in vibrant shades of royal blue and white. Stylistic. Contemporary. Flawlessly executed—except for the finishing touches, the final seal coat. These things he left undone.

Behind the flowers, a few photos of Ethan are propped against the wall. I recognize one instantly. The black-and-white photo that ran in the school paper just a few weeks ago. Ethan leaning back against the mural, his face turned as if studying some point off camera.

Something tightens in my chest. The photographer would have stood right here, crouching low for a close-up, then stepping back for a wider angle shot. I see Ethan's face as if through the camera lens. Those striking features, that clear hypnotic gaze.

The other photos are group shots from his sophomore year. The year he rose up the social ladder. A couple of faces in the photos look familiar—I recognize Carmen's friends, who would have been seniors that year.

As I step closer, I notice the notes tucked in among the flowers.

RIP E.T.

We will always remember you.

"E.T." The initials he penned at the bottom of every sketch, every drawing, every mural he deemed "finished." A process that involved endless touch-ups and revisions until his exacting standards were met.

You told me you'd be here! I silently shout. *We were just starting over.*

But the words begin and end in my head and there is no answer. Only a sort of hollowness.

Thunder rumbles. A sudden gust of wind kicks up the dust.

I glance at the darkening sky and notice a few people

around me studying the flowers, the photos, the notes. Their faces are tight and drawn, like it hurts to look, hurts to remember.

Others pass by without stopping. Merely glancing over with mild curiosity, as if wondering, *Who was Ethan Travvers, anyways?*

Another gust of wind. A raindrop hits the side of my face. Any minute, the late bell will ring. I should get going.

As I step back from the mural, I notice something fluttering. A long black cape.

"Jayden?" I say, my voice rising, as I turn. I didn't know how much I needed to see him until now.

Jayden Harris was the guy with the long locs and monobrow tossing grapes to Bea that day I passed their picnic table during lunch. He and Bea seemed to be Ethan's closest friends. When Ethan started spending his lunches in the graphic arts room instead of at their picnic table, they'd stop by at least once a week. If Ethan wasn't in one of his silent moods, they'd pull up chairs around his workstation and talk about Bea's band, or the cars Jayden was working on at his uncle's shop, or whose party was happening that weekend.

Bea never attempted to include me in these conversations, but Jayden always did.

I glance at him now, standing with his hands stuffed in the pockets of his black jeans, his heavy locs bundled and pulled over one shoulder, and that familiar long black cape tied around his neck. Ethan had mentioned once that Jayden had made the varsity football team as a kicker his sophomore year. Then had to quit the team to work when his parents split. It hardly seemed fair.

Jayden's brown eyes slide to mine and I feel a small flicker of warmth at his nod. For a moment, the loneliness breaks and this is our pain. Our loss.

The late bell rings as the first splatters of rain streak the photos and stain the notes. I wish now for Roger's umbrella. For something I can hold up over these pictures, these notes, these memories. Keep them whole and safe.

The way I wish I could have kept Ethan whole and safe. But didn't.

9

IT WAS LAST October, the day after I saw Ethan at the picnic table with his friends during lunch. According to my calendar, I was supposed to go straight home after school to take an SAT practice test and then work on my UC applications.

Focus was key. Mom had wanted to sign me up with a college admissions counselor back in August. The same frowning, nit-picking, middle-aged lady who'd helped Carmen when she was in my shoes two years ago. I had managed to put it off for the last couple of months. Though just barely. Now the pressure to sign up was back.

I headed toward the bike cage after my last class. However, I wasn't planning on going straight home.

Exhaling shakily, I reached up to adjust my low ponytail for what felt like the tenth time. It'd taken me so long to pick out my outfit that morning—a new white blouse, my favorite sky-blue cardigan, and the one pair of jeans that made my legs look really good—that I ran out of time for everything else.

I still couldn't quite believe it. *Ethan Travvers* had invited me to bike downtown with him. Sure, it was for a school thing, the orchestra shirts. But it was just me, just him. Right?

A sudden image popped into my head of Lucy waiting

at the bike cage in penny loafers and another embroidered "message" sweater.

Did he invite her too?

I didn't like that thought one bit. Besides, Lucy didn't even own a bike. Her mom picked her up and dropped her off—

"Hey."

I looked up to find myself staring into green-gold eyes framed by tousled light brown hair. That tanned skin, those high cheekbones, that barely-there smile. He was wearing what I was beginning to realize was his trademark style—gray shirt and dark-wash jeans.

"Hey," I heard myself say, my voice somehow coming out calm and collected. The exact opposite of how I felt. "Nice bike." I nodded toward his older-style road bike with its thin tube frame and brown handlebar tape. It looked almost vintage.

"It gets me places," Ethan said, shrugging in that casual, easy way I'd always associated with the Populars. "You heading in to get yours?"

I nodded, my stomach fluttering under his clear, steady gaze.

I felt that gaze follow me, curious and assessing, as I made my way into the bike cage. It almost seemed like he was trying to place me somewhere in his mind.

"Now *that*," Ethan said as I wheeled my bike out, "is a nice bike."

I bit my lip, glancing down at the sleek, white frame. Next to his bike, it seemed a little flashy, a little too modern.

I had wanted a lightweight carbon fiber road bike for a long time, and it wasn't until my sixteenth birthday that my parents finally bought me one. It even had a special mount for my violin case. I *loved* this bike.

"Eh," I said, trying and failing to emulate his off-handed shrug as I swung onto my bike. "It gets me places."

"Good," Ethan said, swinging onto his bike. "Because we're about to go places."

"Places like . . . ?" I asked as we wove our way through the parking lot, a treacherous minefield with all the new student drivers.

"Old, converted warehouses with screen-printing equipment inside?" Ethan offered. His brows were raised as he glanced over at me, as if daring me to follow.

For a second, I felt myself pause. The demands of my calendar pushing to the front of my mind. I had told him I'd come, but maybe this wasn't such a good idea after all—

Ethan was still looking my way.

Exhaling, I dropped my gaze to the cozy space between his bike and mine. Maybe, just this time, I could be more like Carmen, less like me.

"Well," I said, nodding at Ethan. "Lead on."

I feel my chest ache now at this memory that leads to all the other memories. His bike, my bike. All the miles of greenbelts and bike lanes we traversed, sometimes riding side by side, sometimes riding one just in front of the other. It was always better together.

There are only a few stragglers in the open halls, half-jogging as the rain begins to fall fast and hard. Soon, it is drumming on the roofs, spilling through the gutters, pooling on the pavement. The smell of wet earth rises, pungent and intoxicating. I breathe in deeply, trying to ease the ache in my chest.

One day, I remind myself. *I can do one day at a time.*

But even as I think this, I feel Ethan's absence all around me like a deep chasm, threatening to swallow me whole.

By the time I step through the double doors of the orchestra practice room, everyone is in their seats tuning their instruments. My sneakers squish as I hurry to cross the room, leaving a trail of muddy footprints behind me.

As I hang my damp jacket off the back of my chair to drip-dry, two cellists and a violist break into an impromptu rendition of "The Imperial March." The double bassists jump up, crossing bows. The timpani player films from his phone, giving an animated play by play. I wince at the crack of the bows striking one another, again and again. I try not to think of the damage to the bow hairs, the stick.

I'm still attaching my shoulder rest when Mr. Martinez takes the stand. The room falls silent, everyone darting back to their places.

Beside me, Lucy gets up to walk to the front of the room. Today, her sweater reads GLASS HALF FULL.

Swallowing hard, I lift my violin to my chin.

I suppose everything is a matter of perspective. A glass could be half full or half empty. Either way, there's still something there.

But what if the glass has been shattered, the water spilt?

Whichever way you look at it, there's nothing there.

10

"SEE YOU TOMORROW!" Roger calls as he pulls away from the curb in front of my house.

Tomorrow. I don't want to think about tomorrow, or the next day, or the next. It was hard enough just getting through today.

I step into our large, white-tiled foyer, exhaling as I close the front door behind me. Everywhere I look is immaculate—from the polished ebony living room piano to the position of the decorative pillows on the wide, alabaster couches, to the vacuum lines in the white carpet.

There isn't a speck of dust on Mom's most recent purchase, a long, single-slab, charred wood coffee table. It's a statement piece, immediately drawing the eye when you walk through the door. Expensive furniture that matches Mom's expensive taste.

The house is quiet. I take off my mud-streaked sneakers and head upstairs. At the top landing, I take a right, pausing for just a second in front of Carmen's door.

It's been closed for months, ever since she left for UCLA in September, more than happy to get away, and happy, it seems, to stay away. Out of habit, I reach for her doorknob, resting my fingers lightly on the metal, touching, but not turning. Letting myself imagine for a moment what it would be like to step in and find my sister there.

Though we grew up in the same house with the same parents, Carmen and I have always been different. She's the one with the tall, toned frame, the flawless skin, the designer clothes, the large following. I'm shorter, with not-so-perfect skin, and while I do have a wide array of functional cardigan sweaters, they're nothing to post about.

Carmen and I used to be part of Roger's youth group, but that small world never seemed to be enough for Carmen. She was always finding other friend groups through her volleyball team, the various school clubs she led, the guys she dated.

Growing up, the gap between Carmen and me—in years, in looks, in worlds—was always painfully obvious. She was leagues ahead of me and I had no hope of ever catching up.

But somehow, late at night, when my insomnia used to keep me up, the gap didn't seem quite so obvious. I'd find myself standing in front of her door in one of my Hello Kitty pajama sets, rapping lightly, feeling like all my worries and fears were going to suffocate me. Wishing I could just sleep and knowing I couldn't.

"Come in," she'd say, as if expecting me.

I'd climb into her messy bed and we'd pretend it was a lifeboat and the cluttered floor was the sea. We were safe as long as we stayed in the boat. Even when Carmen turned sixteen and I was fourteen, we still pretended her bed was a boat.

"So, what's keeping you up?" she'd ask, and I'd tell her. It was easy to tell her things at night, especially in the bed-boat.

When I first met Ethan back in October, Carmen was the first person I wanted to call. I pulled her contact up on my phone, already imagining her voice on the other end of the line saying "So, tell me. Is he *fire?*"

It was our little game, Fire or Ash. We started it while sitting in the airport on a family vacation to Hawaii. When one of us spotted someone really, really good-looking, we'd nudge the other and whisper, "*Fire.*" If the other disagreed, she'd say, "*Ash.*"

We hardly ever disagreed when playing our game.

Now that Ethan's gone, Carmen's still the first person I want to call. But I didn't call her back in October and I don't call her now.

Like Ethan, she also disappeared, vanished. Not suddenly. But slowly, deliberately, until it seemed by the time she left for college, she'd become completely invisible. There, but not there.

Looking back, she started closing herself off from me at the start of her senior year. She still listened while I rambled on in the bed-boat, but shared less and less about herself. I knew she was busy with volleyball, piano, her leadership positions with Honor Society and Model United Nations, working with that nit-picky college admissions counselor. Between all her various activities, she was almost never home. On the rare occasion she was, she would lock herself in her room to work on her laptop.

I remember walking down the hall at night, standing at her door. But every time I lifted my hand to knock, a paralyzing fear gripped me. This thought that instead of inviting me in, Carmen would ask me to leave.

I knew there was something else on her mind. A problem. Something she wasn't telling me. Didn't *want* to tell me. I just couldn't imagine what.

Things were better then, at home. The tension and heaviness around the growth of Dad's startup had finally eased into hopeful optimism. We were riding high on the news that his business was attracting investors, expanding. Even Grandma—a highly successful real estate investor whose exacting standards were impossible to meet—seemed to acknowledge that things were, indeed, looking up.

"Phase two," Rich dubbed it as he sat at our dinner table, gesturing with his hands, his gold wedding band catching the light. Building a picture for us of what would be, this castle in the air.

Rich had come highly recommended a year and a half prior: USC business alum, finance position at a high-profile corporation, and two successful startups. He had drive, creativity, and connections. Not to mention a decent golf game. All things that Dad had told us he was looking for in a business partner.

Rich had also become part of the family. Regularly gracing our dinner table with his loud voice, shaved head, tall muscular frame, and pastel smedium polos. Never missing my violin recitals or Carmen's volleyball matches.

Things were good and likely only going to get better for our family. I wanted to believe the picture Rich built with his hands. I only wondered why Carmen did not seem so optimistic.

Dropping my fingers from Carmen's doorknob, I turn and head down the hall to my room. I close my door behind me, but I still feel it, a heaviness seeping into me.

It's the weight of Carmen's absence, the memory of her presence. The harsh sound of her yelling and of Mom yelling back. The twisted look on her face so warped with anger.

The front door slamming, her car starting. Any excuse to get away.

Carmen's been on academic probation since spring quarter of last year. Then lost her athletic scholarship during summer session.

She went back to UCLA in September and was supposed to come home for Thanksgiving, but texted Mom an hour before her flight saying she wasn't coming. A few weeks later, she canceled her trip home for Christmas, too.

Reaching for my phone, I scroll Carmen's socials, like I've done so many times before. The Carmen I see is not the Carmen I remember. Her long black hair is bleached blond. She seems darker, broodier, with a steely hardness in her eyes that I don't recognize.

Setting my phone aside, I power on my laptop and try to catch up on the work I missed yesterday. But I can't seem to settle in, settle down. There's a familiar flutter in my chest, that old feeling of worry and fear that used to keep me up at nights. I try to push it down, push it away. But the feeling only grows stronger.

You should have told Ethan—an admonition rises, unbidden—*how you felt.*

I close my eyes, my fingers gripping the edge of my Copenhagen desk. There were so many times I could have told him, but didn't. And now he'll never know.

I draw in a sharp breath. Count the steps between my room and Carmen's door on the exhale. This path I've taken on so many nights, climbing out of the sea of my thoughts and into the bed-boat.

11

I HATE WHEN people define their relationship as "complicated." What does that even *mean*? Is it a low-commitment, ambiguous friendship with potential? Or is it something cyclical with breakups and makeups happening every few weeks? Or is it simply a placeholder in which feelings are never spoken out loud?

As last October rolled into November, I found myself wondering more and more whether Ethan and I were "complicated."

He'd asked for my number after that first trip to the screen-printing shop downtown. Texted me a link to some sample comic strips he'd drawn—*The Squirrel Chronicles*—featuring Frenzy, a hyperactive and noble squirrel.

I need the rest of this, I'd texted back, already hooked. **Now.**

The Squirrel Chronicles had a part one *and* a part two. I devoured them both.

Soon after, we started messaging throughout the day, then video calling most nights. We met at my locker in between most periods. Sometimes, we'd bike home from school together, making a pit stop at the donut shop for a dozen donut holes or at the gourmet grocery for smoothies.

Having only traded shy, awkward smiles with guys of

interest prior to this, I was surprised at how easy it was to slip into these routines with Ethan.

In Mom's book, these interactions (or at least the ones she knew about) were more than enough to put me on notice of breaking an MBR. Preliminary restrictions were implemented: checking in with her when I got home from school, limitations on video calls.

I knew I was pushing the boundaries of my regimented life. Deviating from the activities on my color-coded schedule. I traded time working on my college essays and studying for the SATs to bike the trail along Putah Creek with Ethan, or stay on the phone with him for another thirty minutes. I even turned down Mom's offer to sign up with the college admissions counselor.

"Rich-people fluff," Ethan had declared, when I expressed my reservations about Mom's offer. "You're smart. You're already figuring it out."

It felt good that at least *someone* had confidence in me.

Even though Ethan didn't share the details of his past, I felt like I was getting to know him—he hated coffee, he couldn't care less about getting a driver's license, he preferred granola bars over candy bars, and if he could have a pet, it'd be a squirrel named Frenzy.

During class, I thought about what it would be like to have the weight of his arm around my shoulder, the pressure of those perfect lips on mine. But more than that, I wanted words, defining words.

I kept hoping we would talk about it—what we were or what we weren't. But he never brought it up. The one time I tried to broach the subject, I clammed up, my pulse racing and face flushing before I even got to the question.

Ethan was busy that fall, consumed with the new school mural—his largest yet. The steps of the process intrigued me. Everything from the initial sketch to the integration of themes to the development of the vision. Creating something that didn't exist before. It was a new concept for me.

My violin teacher, Mr. Bergamaschi, had wanted me to do more composing—learning to write and perform something original. But I'd never been interested, preferring instead to play and interpret the pieces already written by the prolific composers of the past.

To me, watching Ethan create was like witnessing the composition of a concerto.

It was lunch and I was sitting beside Ethan as he worked on the design of the mural in the graphic arts room. I had just pulled up the string quartet's practice and performance schedule on my laptop when the door to the room slapped open.

Bea's combat boots squeaked against the tile floor as she made her usual dramatic entrance. Entirely unnecessary in my opinion.

"So, is this mural thing, like, your whole life now?" Bea had said, walking straight up to Ethan's workstation. It was rare, her showing up without Jayden. "The picnic table is wondering when all this"—Bea waved a dismissive hand at the image on Ethan's monitor—"is going to be over."

That's what she called their lunch group—"the picnic table." Like they were one unit, and that unit didn't include me.

Ethan raised a brow. "Really? An inanimate object is wondering?"

"You know what I mean," Bea said, unamused. "Did you

get my message? Jayden and I have been trying to reach you, but"—she leaned over Ethan's monitor and grabbed his phone—"you're not checking *this*."

Ethan tried to snatch his phone back, but Bea pulled it just out of reach.

"Bea," he said, his voice tired, "I don't have time for this."

"You don't have time for anything," Bea snapped. "Except hanging out here, doing all these projects for the school, hoping they'll overlook—"

Ethan cut Bea off with a sharp look.

As they stared each other down, I couldn't help but notice the electricity crackling between them. It seemed almost familiar. Like I was getting a glimpse of all the other fights they'd had over the course of their friendship. This history between them.

"So, you haven't told her." Bea glanced over as if noticing me for the first time. "Don't you think—"

"I've got work to do," Ethan said quickly, turning back to the monitor.

"Right. Work," Bea said, and for a second it seemed like she was going to contest that statement. But instead, she sighed, her shoulders dropping. "Well," she said, her gaze sliding toward me, like I was partly to blame, "I'll leave you to it then." Setting his phone on the desk, she walked out, her boots squeaking the whole way back to the door.

In the sudden silence, I looked at Ethan beside me, his brow furrowed, lips compressed, editing the image on the computer. By that point, I was used to studying his every gesture, his every look, his every word. Sometimes it was okay to ask certain questions and other times it was taboo. I knew now wasn't the time to press, but still—

"What did she mean," I began, finding the words thick on my tongue. Afraid that whatever this was, it could change the way I saw him. "About the school—"

Ethan shook his head, a warning.

"But—" I hated that he wasn't even looking at me.

"*Leave it*, Nina." His voice was cold, a steely hardness in his eyes.

12

IT'S BEEN A week since Ethan died.

I hear people talking about him in the halls, during second period physics and fourth period government. I catch snatches of stories, like everyone wants to have some claim to knowing him, even if it was only in passing.

I don't join in their conversations, but I don't try to avoid them either. I have my own memories, my own questions. I'm getting used to the sudden hush, the turning of heads when they notice me.

Instead of taking notes in class, I dissect my past interactions and conversations with Ethan. As if somewhere within those afternoons in the graphic arts room and later outside in the fickle fall weather as he painted the school mural, I should have picked up on his pain.

My steps slow as I approach the locker room for sixth period, PE. Alas, years of dodging physical ed. credits, thinking I could take both symphony orchestra and chamber orchestra semester after semester, have finally caught up with me.

The locker room is wall-to-wall sophomores. Everyone here seems so *young*, like there are ten years between us instead of only two. Twenty different conversations fill the air with all kinds of unnecessary laughing and screaming.

I keep to my corner, keep to myself. Change into the school-issued gym clothes—bulky gray sweater and black sweatpants that don't fit me at all. I try to roll up the waist band, pull down the sleeves. But I still look heavy, shapeless.

I file out into the cold for roll call, hoping I'll recognize somebody, anybody. But I don't.

Stretches. Push-ups. Crunches.

Set after set after set.

I'm a musician, *not* an athlete.

The shrill blast of a whistle. Now we're in the weight room with its whitewashed brick walls and bare concrete floors. I'm lying on my back, a strangling pressure against my chest. The fluorescent lights above me are cold, sterile. Like a morgue—

"You going to lift, or what?"

My bench press partner, a frizzy-haired sophomore, glances down at her watch and then across the room. She surreptitiously snaps her gum for the hundredth time. It smells faintly like artificial watermelon. Yuck.

"How many sets was that?" I ask.

"One." She doesn't even bother to look at the clipboard. Snaps her gum again.

"Can you check? I thought I did two."

"Nope." She still doesn't look. "Just one."

I think about ripping out that wad of watermelon gum and mashing it into her hair. But instead, I reposition my grip on the bar, feeling the roughness of the steel against my soft, uncalloused palm.

Wasn't this supposed to be 80 percent mental and 20 percent physical?

If so, I can do this. I just need to close my eyes and

visualize, the way I do before every violin performance, running through each piece in my head, the fingering, the bowing, everything perfect—

"Set two." Gum snap above me. "Zero reps."

"Okay, okay." Planting my feet, I throw my weight behind the bar until it reluctantly lifts, one inch, then two. I keep pushing, up from my legs, my chest. It's surprising how hard it is just to bench press the bar. I can't imagine what it's like with actual weights attached.

"You . . . almost got it."

I force my elbows to straighten, feeling the shake in my arms before lowering.

"That's one, two—" My bench press partner stares down at me, a bored expression on her face.

I gasp, sweat popping on my forehead. This shouldn't be legal.

"Three . . ."

The florescent lights flicker. For a second, the weight benches look like gurneys. On the one beside me, I think I see a body bag. Ethan's.

My stomach lurches, the bar twists.

"Hey!" My bench press partner exclaims. "You okay?" She makes a grab for the bar, the clipboard clattering to the ground.

"I feel—" I sit up, the room spinning, tilting. "Sick."

Clapping a hand over my mouth, I burst through the nearest exit door. It opens to the west side of campus, across from the agriculture building, the auto shop. A couple students mill around, glancing over as I stagger to the nearest bathroom.

Bile burns up the back of my throat. The stall door whaps

shut behind me as I double over and heave into the toilet. But nothing comes out.

I wait, my face flushed, stomach gurgling, willing it to come.

A toilet flushes two stalls down. I hear the heavy tread of boots across the bathroom floor and water splashing in the sink. The air dryer runs, shuts off, runs again. Then, silence.

I drag in a ragged breath, another, wishing I didn't have to go back to the weight room, the classrooms, the bell schedule. This world where I'm here, but Ethan's not.

I just want relief, something to make this all better instead of worse—

It gets worse.

"You." Bea turns from the sink as I exit the stall, her muscular body swiveling, kohl-lined eyes narrowed, accusing.

A familiar bitterness rises in my throat. She was the reason Ethan and I went our separate ways in December. Telling him we'd never work when she didn't even know me. And somehow, he believed her.

"Yeah. Me." I edge past her to the sink, glancing down at her knuckles which are crusted with scabs. "What about it?"

Her gaze shifts from my wilted ponytail and the dark circles under my eyes, to the bulky PE clothes with N. YEUNG written across the chest in permanent marker.

"I always wondered what Ethan saw in you," she says slowly. "Why he'd bother to start things when he already had someone else."

Someone else.

Something stutters in my chest. I stare at the water running over my hands, the soapy foam slipping down the drain. The parties she and Jayden would mention, the small concert venues her band often played at. I was never invited to those places.

Was there someone there, someone outside the fence lines of our bikes, the mural, the orchestra shirts? Someone who also understood his mood swings? Someone else he liked to stay on the phone with and message throughout the day, never defining things—

"I wouldn't know," I hear myself say, the force in my voice surprising me. This was just another angle she was taking, another stab at trying to make me feel irrelevant.

"Of course, you wouldn't." Bea steps toward me, tall in her combat boots. Like she's the authority on all things Ethan. "He was always good at keeping secrets. Letting people see just enough to believe what he needed them to believe."

I shake my head as I rub my hands beneath the air dryer, letting the heat ripple over my skin. My mind wavers. He wasn't like that. She was just making things up, hoping I'd bite.

"So." I turn from the air dryer, brows raised. "What was it he needed *you* to believe?"

Bea's face seems to pale, to blank. But in the next second, the look's gone.

"Nothing," she sneers, stepping toward me, her breath—which smells like peach gummies—hot in my face.

I edge back a step, then another. The metal rim of the trash can digs into my hip.

"I knew him. But you"—she jabs a finger at my chest and I get an up-close view of her scabs—"you didn't know him *at all*."

The trash can tips, crashing to the floor.

13

I SIT AT a small desk in a far corner of the library after school, my stats homework laid out in front of me.

But instead of calculating probabilities, I'm scrolling through Ethan's memorial page on my phone. This seemingly endless string of photos and messages posted by people I don't know.

He was always good at keeping secrets. Bea's words to me in the bathroom earlier.

Secrets.

Like the way he never talked about his past. Or how he'd cut Bea off when she'd criticized him for doing all those projects for the school hoping they'd overlook . . . whatever it was.

That strange jolt I felt that first day I met Ethan outside the school library—like I'd pricked my finger or stepped on hot pavement in bare feet. How many others had felt the same way, meeting him for the first time or the hundredth time?

I feel my chest constrict and my head grow light.

I can still see us on our bikes, still hear the whiz of our tires against the pavement. It was always better together. And I *know* he felt it too.

The orchestra shirts were finally distributed in November,

before Thanksgiving. Almost overnight, it seemed everywhere you walked on campus, you saw Ethan's distinctive design: bold white lines against black, DHS ORCHESTRA in old stone lettering, narrow, across the chest.

"Where's *your* shirt?" Ethan had asked when he saw me after school the next day wearing my usual blouse and cardigan combo with a light winter coat.

"Didn't buy one," I replied.

"That's a shame," Ethan said, as we headed to the bike racks. "Considering who designed it."

I rolled my eyes. "Well, I hope you're not offended or anything."

"Oh, I am." He threw me an accusatory look. "*Very* offended."

"You'll have to talk to my mom then," I shot back, stooping to unlock my bike. "She doesn't approve of T-shirts. She thinks they're too informal."

"Informal. Really?" Ethan frowned as he pulled his bike from the rack and swung over the frame. "As in reserved for dirty housework and picking up dog poop?"

I laughed. "Something like that."

We biked fast through the park that day, under the heavy canopy of trees changing color, past the wooden play structure and the arts center. We switched to low gear to ride up the long bridge that crossed the tracks. Then switched gears again before coasting down the other side.

"So," Ethan said as we neared the intersection where he would usually make a right to go to his house and I would make a left to go to mine. "I got you something. A present. If you have time to stop by." His voice was normal, casual. But his body was tense and he couldn't seem to meet my eye.

"A present," I repeated, intrigued and suspicious at the same time. He'd never gotten me anything before and my birthday was still months away.

"Yeah," he said, turning finally to look at me.

I drew in a breath. Those high cheekbones, those perfect lips and green-gold eyes. I could never get tired of looking.

But as I glanced down at my watch, I felt the familiar pull of tension between what I should do and what I wanted to do. It was two and a half miles between the golf course community where I lived and the older duplex community where Ethan lived. I had to be home in exactly twenty minutes for my private violin lesson. At Mr. Bergamaschi's exorbitant hourly rate, I couldn't afford to be late.

But Ethan was inviting me to his *house,* saying he had something for me.

"Five minutes," I relented, telling myself this could be it. The moment where we finally stopped being "complicated" and defined things. "That's all I got."

Ten minutes later, Ethan was still rifling through his closet, his dresser, shuffling through the pile of worn paperbacks on his desk—mostly science fiction—his mood darkening with each passing second.

I tried not to notice, focusing instead on the black-and-white sketches he had pinned to the walls—geometric patterns that formed a picture within a picture. I looked for his trademark signature, "E.T.," at the bottom of each sketch.

"It's fine. I'll just get it from you tomorrow," I offered, checking my watch for the fifth time.

"*No,*" Ethan snapped, motioning for me to stay.

I wanted to explain, about Mr. Bergamaschi, my weekly

private lessons. But I worried that mentioning my music, my schedule, would just irritate him more. Glancing again at my watch, I swallowed the words I wanted to say.

"Here."

Ethan shoved a flat, rectangular package into my hands. It felt soft, flexible. I quickly removed the paper wrapping.

A black T-shirt. DAVIS HIGH SCHOOL ORCHESTRA in light blue lettering framed by white baby wings. Flying music notes, a bald eagle soaring into the sunset—all the ideas Lucy and I had pitched to Ethan that first day we met at the library.

"Gross."

Ethan smiled, his mood instantly lightening. "You're welcome."

He stood in front of me in his trademark fitted gray shirt and dark jeans, his arms folded across his chest. I wished I could memorize that smile, this moment. I was in his house, his room, with *him*. Suddenly, I couldn't think about anything other than that.

"You know," I said, bending to shove the shirt into my backpack. I needed a second to hide the flush that had risen to my face. "This definitely could have waited until tomorrow."

"But you didn't have an *orchestra* shirt," Ethan countered, stepping closer and letting his arms drop to his sides. "I had to fix that."

"Never mind the fact that I don't wear T-shirts," I reminded him.

"This one could be the exception," Ethan said, raising his brows. "It's got *baby wings*—your favorite."

"Words elude me." I reached for my backpack, mentally calculating the time it'd take me to bike home in high gear.

"You mean, words like 'thank you'?"

He stood so close, looking down at me. I caught the light, clean scent of his cologne and felt the solidity of his presence. I could hear our breaths, loud in the sudden silence. I tilted my face up as he leaned toward me—

The front door opened and footsteps approached. A thin, angular woman with a gray bob and a worn leather briefcase manifested in his doorway.

"Mom." Ethan pulled back, his shoulders instantly stiff, his tone guarded. "This is Nina. Nina, this is my mom, Katheryn."

The woman's pale blue eyes, small behind her rimless spectacles, shifted toward me.

"Hi, Mrs. Travvers—" I hazarded, still flustered. The pull between us, Newton's law of universal gravitation drawing together two objects. The way he'd leaned in, I knew he'd felt it too.

She blinked, her gaze hostile. "It's *Doctor*," she corrected.

I felt heat rise to my face, an apology forming on my lips. But then she was gone, her footsteps fading down the narrow hall. A door opened and shut.

"I need to go," I said, turning to Ethan, my face still hot.

He nodded, following me out the door where I unlocked my bike and pushed it down the short walkway to the curb.

I wanted him to say something about our almost-kiss. For him to explain his mom's brusqueness and assure me it wasn't personal. But I already knew he wouldn't. Ethan wasn't one for explanations, for himself or for others.

All this time, I'd been wishing, wanting words to define our relationship. But what if they never came? What if I only had his actions to read instead?

The gift, the almost-kiss . . . maybe they were his way of telling me the three words I needed to hear.

14

I HEAR THEM before I see them. The Jolly Twosome.

Fresh out of their Honor Society meeting and now wandering through the school library. Having some kind of debate in hushed library voices.

"Ah," Roger remarks, rounding the corner with Lucy. "So, this is 'The Hideout.'"

I glance up from my phone with Ethan's memorial page pulled up. If I still had my biking privileges, I'd be home by now.

"What happened to texting when Honor Society got out?" I demand, setting my phone on the table, face down.

My mind is still drowning in past memories. Trying to fit Bea's version of Ethan—the one who had *someone else*—with mine.

Everything in me wants to dismiss Bea's claims as just another barb, another dart. Anything to drive Ethan and me apart. I always found it strange, her sense of entitlement over Ethan. Like she knew him better, best.

I'd like to think I knew him too, as well, maybe better. The only problem is, my version of Ethan would never have climbed the safety fence on the bridge. Never would have jumped. Would Bea's version have done it?

"The library's not that big." Roger shrugs his skinny shoulders. "We figured we could find you."

"Not 'we,'" Lucy clarifies, her tone apologetic. "Just him."

So that was what they were debating.

"The youth group's having a potluck this Friday at Traci's," Roger announces as we push through the library's heavy glass doors. "You should come."

I remember going to Traci Campos's house back at the start of senior year. Hanging out with her on the big tire swing in her backyard as we watched Roger attempt to build a fire in the fire pit. A pitiful pile of smoldering sticks until he decided to add lighter fluid. Burned his eyebrows straight off.

But too much has happened since then. It doesn't feel right to just show up again.

"Everyone asks about you," Lucy chimes in as we head toward the parking lot. "Especially on Catan nights."

For a second, I feel a twinge of regret. I'm *really* good at board games. I've missed playing with the group.

"I can't make it," I hear myself say. It's the response I've perfected after months of being with Ethan.

"Why not?" Of course Roger won't let this go. "You have something else going on?"

"No." He knows this.

"Then you should come."

I shake my head. "No." From the body bag in the weight room to the confrontation in the bathroom, I've had more than enough for today. I just want to get off campus. Go home. Be alone.

We're almost to Roger's car when it happens.

His neck swivels to the left, his mouth dropping open

in a wide grin. The next thing I know, he's waving like he's trying to flag down a rescue ship.

"Hey, hey!" Roger shouts to a large group of people two rows of cars down.

"Keys," I demand, holding one palm up before he can drag me over there to socialize.

"But Nina," Roger protests, pointing across the parking lot. "It's Rochelle and Traci and Cameron—"

"Keys," I repeat.

Roger makes a sad face, bottom lip out. "Okie doke, Nina," he says, handing them over. "We'll be right back."

Lucy's riding with us today, so I climb into the back seat of Roger's car and slam the door. Minutes pass. The cloud cover breaks and the afternoon sun slants directly through the back window. A half-eaten bag of potato chips crunches under my left shoe. Something lumpy digs into my back—a pair of old gym socks.

Gagging, I reach for the window crank, but the handle is jammed.

I watch Roger two rows down, his long arms flailing as he recounts an episode from the school cafeteria. Something about stewed carrots and tots. I hear Lucy's high-pitched laugh above the others.

I swallow hard, remembering being a part of that group. Everyone trying to one-up Roger's stories. Laughing so hard it hurts.

Two sets of footsteps finally approach the car. Roger and Lucy walking hand-in-hand in their matching white Etsy sweaters with SMILE embroidered, large, across the front.

Something tightens in my chest and I look down into my lap.

I'm happy for Roger. Glad he found someone just like him. Still, I can't get used to the idea of him and Lucy. The idea of my friend Roger with anyone.

Is that how Bea felt? Maybe, like her, I feel entitled because I knew Roger first. Because I was there for him three and a half years ago when his dad was rushed to the hospital. There through the misdiagnosis, the premature discharge, the massive heart attack. I was the one holding his little brothers as his mom wept, her tears pooling on the hospital's tile floor. I was there, praying the same prayers over and over, hoping until there was nothing left to hope for. Only goodbye.

"Can't lie, I'm pumped for the sledding trip Saturday," Roger says as Annabel roars to life. "Rochelle knows a good spot in Truckee, very secluded, and most importantly—*free.*"

"We'll need to bring gloves, snow pants, tubes, saucers . . ." Lucy pulls out her phone, making notes.

"How do you feel about sledding, Nina?" Roger glances at me in the rearview mirror, his smile broad. "You should come with us. It'll be fun."

I think of flying down a hill with no brakes, no pedals. Just the pull of gravity.

"I don't feel up for that."

"What about the potluck at Traci's?"

"Probably not." My words are clipped, forced. Maybe Roger can bounce back from his tragedy, but I can't even begin to see a way through mine.

"Nina," Roger chides, his tone sober.

"What?"

"Nina."

"*What?*"

"You. Need. To. Come."

I stare at the center console, where Roger's fingers are intertwined with Lucy's. Comfortable, secure. Like they belong together, the way I wanted Ethan and me to belong together.

"No," I say finally.

Roger sighs. "Well, there's always next time."

Except there isn't. Not for me, not for Ethan. Not for everything I'd hoped we could be.

15

A STORM BLOWS through Wednesday night, with more storms in the forecast.

I wear my plaid rain boots and my navy rain jacket with the deep hood to school. I pass Ethan's memorial on my way to first period orchestra. The wind and rain have stained the photos, soaked the bits of paper, and scattered the silk flowers.

I chase down every flower I can find and stack them again in neat piles.

But the next morning, it's gone. All of it. The area swept and tidied. I knew this was coming. But still, it feels like too much, too soon.

When I get home, I go to my closet and reach way back to pull out my one T-shirt. Black, with DAVIS HIGH SCHOOL ORCHESTRA in light blue lettering framed by white baby wings.

I crush it to my face and breathe in. Deep, deep. Needing to feel Ethan here, with me.

It smells as new as the day he gave it to me. I see us standing together in his room. I tilt my face up as he leans in—

Why did it have to *end* like this?

I throw the shirt across my room, a sob breaking out of

me, loud and violent. I wish it was as simple as "I loved him and he loved me." But instead, it's all these *questions* and *doubts* and *memories* . . .

I think back to that last week in November. The week I felt so overwhelmed with the UC application deadline looming, getting the string quartet prepped for our highest-paid gig, finishing my paper for government, and studying for a physics test.

I'd been brushing Lucy off every time she asked about scheduling quartet practice. But as we left first period orchestra, she wasn't letting it go.

"How's Thursday night look?" Lucy pressed, walking with me to my locker even though her next class was in the opposite direction.

I'd pulled up the color-coded schedule on my phone trying to find one empty slot. Thursday, Thursday . . . I felt like I was missing something on my calendar that happened on Thursday nights.

"Isn't that activity night for youth group?" I finally asked. "Roger hates when people miss."

"It's not like you've gone in the last couple of months," Lucy said, raising her brows.

"Right." I didn't want to get into that. "Thursday night is fine," I answered, anything to get her to go away. "I'll send a message to the quartet. We'll meet at my place at seven."

Which meant I had to finish my government paper after school, the time I had blocked out to work on my UC applications—

"Hey!" I snapped, my tone much sharper than I intended. "Can you move?" I needed to get my physics textbook and some guy was leaning against my locker.

"Why? Am I in your way?" Ethan looked up from his phone, his hazel eyes locking with mine.

I blinked, my breath catching hard. He looked so entirely different with short hair it made my head spin. His light brown hair seemed blonder, his features bolder with a taper fade. He was taller somehow, less approachable. Ethan, but not Ethan, at the same time.

"As a matter of fact, you are in my way, *dork*." Elbowing him roughly aside, I stepped up to work the combination on my locker.

"Tsk, tsk, Nina. Has anyone told you your manners need some work?"

I ignored his comment. "When did you decide to get a haircut?" I demanded. In the last two months of *whatever we were*, it never occurred to me he could have other looks.

"Last night." Ethan ran his fingers over the back of his shorn head, cringing slightly. "Didn't have much of a choice."

Did Katheryn force him to get a haircut?

"It looks good." I grabbed my physics textbook, knowing the word was a complete understatement. Forced or not, the haircut suited him.

"You're just saying that."

"*Or maybe*," I said, slapping my locker door shut and turning to face him, "it's the truth."

A sharp whistle cut the hallway din and heads turned our way.

"Nice cut," Bea smirked, snapping a military salute as she passed. Ignoring me, as usual.

Ethan's neck reddened and I wondered how much he cared what she thought of him.

"So." I shifted the textbook in my arm, wanting his

attention back on me. More than a week had passed since the almost-kiss in his room. I kept hoping, waiting for us to pick up where we'd left off. "What's the occasion?"

"An award ceremony at the university." Ethan tugged at his shirt collar, loosening an invisible tie. "My mom's getting recognized for her research. Formal thing. Stuffy dinner. You know the type."

"I'm surprised you didn't find a way to get out of it."

"I'm running out of options these days."

"How so?" I studied him, wondering. Ethan's lows seemed to be getting more frequent—the spans of radio silence, abruptly ending conversations, brooding alone. Part of me wished he'd tell me what was going on. Another part of me didn't.

"Actually . . . you could come. If you want."

Something stuttered in my chest, even as I realized he'd sidestepped the question. An invitation. Out. With *him*. "To a stuffy 'formal thing'?"

He made a face. "Forget it."

"When is it?" I asked, trying to keep my voice casual. But inside I felt breathless, eager.

"Thursday night."

I felt my stomach sink. Of course it was. I'd have to talk to Lucy, see if we could possibly reschedule—

"Sure. I'll be there." The words came so quickly, so easily, that even Ethan looked surprised.

"I thought you were busy this week." He glanced sideways at me. "College applications and quartet stuff, right?"

He would know. He was the one who convinced me that I didn't need a college admissions counselor. That I was smart enough to do it myself.

"It's fine. I'll figure it out." My voice portrayed a confidence I didn't feel. I was already arranging and rearranging my schedule in my head, trying to see how I could possibly make this all work.

"You sure?" His fingers brushed mine. I felt his skin, rough from working long hours on the school mural. Up on a ladder, a paint palette in one hand and a brush in the other. Trying to get every detail right.

My throat tightened, something quickening in my chest. "Yeah," I heard myself say. "I'm sure."

Now as I cross my room, I pick the black T-shirt off the floor. But instead of hanging it back in my closet, I collapse onto my bed, holding it tight against my chest. The way I wish I could wrap my arms around Ethan and hold him, here, now.

I was so caught up that day with Ethan's new look, my looming deadlines, his invite for me to be his plus one. I didn't press when he sidestepped my question.

But now I wonder. The sharp haircut, Bea's miliary salute. What options was he running out of then?

I think of his mom, Katheryn. Of her cold reception that first day I met her in his room. Of her equally cold reception on the ride to the university function. Had he crossed some kind of line with her? Did she have anything to do with committing Ethan to those art projects for the school?

And what, exactly, does Bea know that I don't?

16

IT'S LATE AFTERNOON by the time I emerge from my room.

I head downstairs and switch on the floor lamp beside the piano, arrange my sheet music on the stand.

My weekly violin lesson with Mr. Bergamaschi is tomorrow afternoon. I'm working on learning Bartók's Violin Concerto No. 2. I'm playing all three movements of the concerto at my senior recital in April. I've already pictured how it will feel performing this concerto on stage. The triumph of mastering such a difficult piece. The applause.

Perhaps Grandma will notice me then.

Black notes across a white page. The unforgiving click of the metronome. I feel the bite of the strings, the pressure I place on my bow as I play each note at half speed, focusing only on fingering. Four measures of the Bartók concerto, four times perfect.

I then repeat the same four measures at three-quarters speed. Four times perfect. It's all about maintaining control. But even though I'm playing the right notes, using the right fingering, the sound is all wrong.

I had trouble with these four measures—this whole section—during my lesson last week. The notes falling flat instead of "singing," the phrasing fragmented instead of "telling a story," as Mr. Bergamaschi put it. If I play any other way than perfect tomorrow, he will pick it apart. Or rather, pick me apart.

I switch off the metronome and play from the beginning of the section. But the music does not resonate, does not translate into emotion. It stays at the surface where I can't taste its sweetness, its power. Just like that first day back in orchestra and every day since.

Setting down my bow, I flip through the sheet music, feeling a growing heaviness as I study the pages and pages of music I still need to learn. It's impossible. Especially without being able to feel the music.

What was I *thinking*? I should have listened to Mr. Bergamaschi when he suggested I pick an easier concerto for my recital. But I had wanted the challenge. Had become obsessed with an old video I'd seen of an incredible violinist playing this piece with a full orchestra. I couldn't get over the way she understood and interpreted the dissonance and edginess of Bartók.

The only problem is, I'm not her. And now it's too late to go back.

"Nina!" Mom comes in through the garage door in a light gray pantsuit, carrying her briefcase and a bag of groceries from the Asian market near her work. "Can you grab the other groceries from the car?"

I set down my violin and head to the garage. As I reach for the two bags in her trunk, I notice a long black mark along the left side wall. A mark my bike must have left on her car that day she picked me up at the bridge.

And she still hasn't mentioned Ethan by name.

Closing the trunk, I carry the bags into the kitchen and help put things away in the fridge, the pantry. There are no snacks, nothing pre-made. It's all ingredients: cans of coconut milk, spices, vegetables, meat, fish.

"Do you think," I begin, glancing at Mom as she ties on an apron and sets a pot of water to boil on the gas range, "I could do the hour lessons with Mr. Bergamaschi, instead of the forty-five-minute lessons? Just for the next month?"

Mom's brow pinches. "The hour lessons," she says, her voice tight, and I can almost see her running the numbers in her head.

"I just need some extra help learning the concerto."

Mom exhales, silent for a moment. "I'll call him," she says finally.

Over the next hour and a half, I force myself to practice. Even though I can't feel the music, I still play. Working on learning the notes, the phrasing, the fingering.

Dad comes home.

I take my seat at the glass dining table. There's lotus soup, thin slices of pan-fried pork chops, a large bowl of green beans sauteed in sesame oil, and a pot of white rice. I wasn't feeling hungry earlier, but now my stomach grumbles.

Mom has changed out of her work clothes, but Dad sits at the table with his dress shirt buttoned all the way up, his tie still knotted at his neck. I can't help but notice the bags under his eyes, the gray in his hair. New, since the startup began to flounder in December.

I scoop some rice into my bowl, add green beans, and then a slice of pork.

My parents' conversation drifts from key performance indicators of the startup to Carmen.

My sister has always embodied achievement and image, the two things that mean everything to our extended family.

Carmen was named MVP for the varsity volleyball team and graduated as high school salutatorian. She then went on to secure a volleyball scholarship at UCLA and pursue a major in microbiology and a minor in entrepreneurship. She even spent a summer interning at Dad's company. She's always stylish, effortlessly beautiful. All things that earned her the spot as Grandma's favorite, the shining example to me and my cousins of what success looks like.

Or rather . . . looked like.

Grandma doesn't know that Carmen has been on academic probation, that she lost her athletic scholarship this year. Two blows my parents have kept secret, Mom making excuses to Grandma for Carmen's glaring absence during Thanksgiving and Christmas.

My parents continue talking as if I'm not even here. Something about Carmen wanting to move out of the on-campus housing.

"I don't know, Vin." Mom sets her bowl of soup down with a clank. "We haven't looked at this place or met the occupants. I'm just not comfortable."

"It's what she wants," Dad counters. He always takes Carmen's side. "It will save us some money and Carmen says she's known these people for a while now."

"From where? Have *you* met them?" Mom's voice is strained. It doesn't help that Carmen doesn't answer Mom's calls anymore.

"She's in college, Melanie," Dad says. "She's allowed to make some decisions."

His side, her side, this same sheet of music played over and over again.

I wish they'd ask about me, how I'm doing, how my senior recital piece is coming, how I'm surviving the horrors of PE. Ask if I'd like to go driving, get more practice hours behind the wheel. I wish they'd acknowledge that Ethan jumped and I shattered.

But they're still talking about Carmen when I get up from the table and take my plate and bowl to the sink.

It's only when the doorbell rings that they finally stop.

17

"COMING THROUGH!" PETER says, dragging his cello case into the tiled foyer and taking off his shoes before stepping on the white carpet.

Mom doesn't allow any shoes past the foyer, a rule she strictly enforces.

"Hey, Nina!"

Madison and then Lucy file in the door with their instrument cases. I hear a car horn beep from the curb. It sounds like Roger's.

Quartet practice is *tonight*? Here? I thought we'd just met—

I shiver as the cold night air rushes through the front door.

"Where are the folding chairs, Nina?" Madison asks as she opens and closes random doors in our hallway, one of Mom's pet peeves.

I close the front door as Mom opens the door to the hall closet. "Chairs are in here," she tells Madison, frowning slightly as she takes in Madison's loungewear—plaid pajama pants paired with an oversized sweatshirt that hits below the knees.

Everyone is bustling around me, setting up chairs in the living room, unfolding music stands, unzipping and unbuckling instrument cases.

I remember a time when I thrived in this flurry of activity. A time when I reviewed playlists days in advance of each quartet practice, solicited votes on various song arrangements, made sure we were well-prepared for every gig, big or small. I even enjoyed doing the balance spreadsheets, tabulating the payments received for each gig along with the costs of our supplies and travel expenses.

But somewhere in the fallout after Ethan and I split in December, I lost that drive. I let things slide. The split was so sudden, so unexpected, that I still find myself reeling at the thought—

"You okay?" Lucy asks, pulling her folding chair closer to mine.

"Yeah," I say, leaning forward to adjust the height of my music stand. "Fine."

"Mr. Martinez says he hasn't been able to get ahold of you."

Right. Because I've been avoiding him, sliding into class just before he calls the orchestra to order and leaving immediately after.

"He's . . . concerned," Lucy continues, her voice low, as Peter and Madison settle into their seats and start to tune their instruments. "He knows you're going through a lot right now."

"I'm fine," I repeat.

"It's okay not to be," Lucy says, her tone vaguely robotic, as if channeling whatever was shared at the mandatory assembly. "You just lost someone important. We all get that. Mr. Martinez said if you wanted to take a break from leading the quartet—"

"*What?*" My body stiffens as I turn to face Lucy. "No!"

"He just thought—"

"I said no. I. Am. Fine."

Lucy opens her mouth as if to refute this, but then reconsiders.

"Nina, we have two gigs on Saturday, right?" Madison asks. "The wedding in the afternoon and the anniversary party that night?"

As the lead, I should know this off the top of my head. But that part of my brain appears to be missing.

"Hang on." I frantically pull up our booking schedule on my phone. It can't be this weekend. We're nowhere near ready. "*Next* Saturday," I say, breathing a sigh of relief. "Not this one."

"What kind of food do you think they'll have at the wedding?" Peter muses, adding more rosin to his bow.

"The kind you're probably allergic to," Madison says. "We don't need a repeat of the arboretum wedding."

"It was just a touch of hives," Peter protests.

"That almost cost us the whole gig," Lucy notes with a pointed look.

Peter slumps.

I clear my throat, consulting my phone for the playlist emailed to me from the bride's wedding planner. "Let's start," I say, forcing confidence into my voice, "with Mendelssohn's 'Wedding March.'"

A shuffling of sheet music, a couple of squeaky starts, and then the rich tones of a familiar piece fill the room.

Music to accompany a walk down an aisle, friends and family rising from the pews. Vows that mark the beginning of something new.

But as we move through the piece, I see a different scene unfold in my head. Friends and family sitting in pews, a closed casket. The eulogy that marks the end of things.

18

IT HAPPENED THE second week of December. I finally heard back from the Young Musicians Intensive, the long wait over.

"Ethan, guess," I prompted as we headed across campus to our lockers. His hair was growing back out, but was still shorter than normal. It made my breath catch every time I looked at him.

He didn't reply. Just kept walking straight ahead with his jaw set and one hand wrapped loosely around the strap of his heavy-duty canvas messenger bag. He was in one of his silent moods. But still, I hoped he'd play along.

"C," he said finally, his tone clipped.

"Ha!" I elbowed him lightly. "I'm not talking about your strategy on standardized testing."

"Enlighten me then," Ethan said, but there was something off about his voice. A subtlety that would bother me were it any other day, any other moment.

"I got in!" I shouted. Part of me wanted to throw my arms up. Do a little dance. Break an MBR about making a scene.

Ethan finally turned toward me, but his eyes were dark and his brow knitted. "What are you talking about?"

"*Young Musicians Intensive.* My application? The recordings I worked on for weeks? You know."

He shrugged. "Bravo."

I bit my lip, stung by his response, but still too worked up to dwell on it. "It's just so surreal." I exhaled slowly, trying to calm the fluttering in my stomach. "I'd hoped, but I didn't think it'd actually happen."

Ethan looked away—no smile, no pat on the back, not even a golf clap. "So that means . . . you're leaving," he said.

"Yeah. I'm going to *Colorado*. For ten whole days. Can you believe it?"

"No." Ethan's voice sounded distant, strange. "I can't."

A tense silence fell between us.

"So," I said, after a moment, "are you going to work on the mural this afternoon?"

"No."

"Why not?" I glanced at him, confused. Just the other day, he'd asked if I could stay with him later after school. That he was entering, in his words, "The Final Push." A concentrated effort to ensure that necessary final touches to the mural were completed to his exacting standards—the mural worthy of his signature.

He shrugged. "Don't feel like it."

"What are you going to do instead?" Perhaps he was thinking we could bike to the park downtown or do a loop around the university.

His hand tightened against the strap of his bag. "Don't know."

I felt a sudden stab of disappointment at the thought of not seeing him after school.

The silence between us seemed to lengthen.

"Did you end up finishing your art portfolio?" I asked, trying to keep the conversation going.

I knew Ethan had been working with the graphic arts teacher to pull together a portfolio for a couple of art and design schools. One in New York and one in Washington.

Ethan frowned. "I'm not . . . doing that anymore."

"I thought you wanted to go."

"I don't." Ethan's face was pinched, hard. "Maybe I'm okay just staying here."

"What do you mean?"

We stood outside the literature building, another one of Ethan's school projects—posters for winter formal—hanging on the wall beside us.

"Not everyone needs to get out of Davis, Nina."

I shook my head, not getting it.

"You'll be at YMI," Ethan said slowly, deliberately. "And then off to some music college after that, right?"

"Yeah. But I'll be back. YMI is only for a week and a half and it will be late summer or early fall before I leave for—"

"Bea was right," Ethan cut in. "It's just history repeating itself. We'd never work."

Never work.

The words hit me hard. I staggered, reeling, trying to catch my breath—

"What are you saying?" My voice was high, tight.

"You. Me." He shrugged. "This."

There was a crashing in my ears, a thousand marbles dropped on a glass floor.

The bell rang. The door to the literature building opened and shut, people rushing, rushing by.

Tears stung my eyes. I stepped forward, but he stepped back.

One moment there, the next, gone.

I'd missed it then, in the freshness of the split. But now, as I head to my locker after lunch, I wonder what he'd meant by history repeating itself. Did someone leave him while he stayed? What did that have to do with me—with us?

Bea's accusation in the bathroom that I didn't know him *at all*. Is she right?

I have to talk to Jayden.

19

I WAIT OUTSIDE the auto shop on the west side of campus as fifth period advanced auto lets out.

I scan all the passing faces, but I don't see Jayden Harris. I haven't seen him since that day we'd stood together in front of Ethan's mural, looking down at the flowers, the notes, the pictures.

Last night, I'd scoured Ethan's memorial page, the local news sources, the school's website. Wanting to find details about Ethan's funeral. A date, a time, a place, so I could be there.

But I couldn't find anything about it.

"Nina?" Jayden walks up to me, his long locs a heavy mass down his back. He's wearing a grease-stained shirt and faded black jeans, his cape bunched up in one hand. "What are you doing here?"

"I—" I swallow, my mouth suddenly dry. "I was actually hoping to find you."

"And so you have," Jayden says, the corners of his lips turning up.

I attempt to smile back, but my face feels stiff. "How are you?" I finally manage, hating the tremble in my voice.

"Holding up," Jayden says. He bunches the cape tighter

in his hands, a furrow forming in the center of his monobrow. "How about you?"

I shake my head. "I don't know." I blink hard, trying to hold back the tears, but they come anyway. "Bad?"

"Yeah." His response is immediate. "I know what you mean."

I swipe at the corners of my eyes, feeling both the warmth of his understanding and the sharp ache of our loss.

"Do you know if there's going to be . . . ?" I can't seem to get the word out. "If there's going to be a . . . ?"

I can't say it. Why can't I just *say* it?

"There won't be a funeral," Jayden answers.

No funeral. Ethan's life unremembered, unfinished. Like a concerto without a finale, the final pages of the sheet music blank.

I shake my head, hating the idea of it. "Why?"

Jayden looks down and away. "It's . . . something you'll have to ask Dr. Travvers."

"But you have some idea, right?" I press, surprised at my own boldness. "Of the reason."

"I have my guesses." Jayden shrugs, kicking absently at a rock. The movement is practiced, fluid, and we both watch as the rock flies off his shoe and drops neatly into the bushes.

I wonder if he misses playing football.

"Anything you can tell me?"

"Depends," Jayden says slowly, his brown gaze sliding back to meet mine.

"On what?" Desperation creeps into my voice, but I don't care. "Just tell me. *Please*."

The warning bell rings for sixth period, but neither of us moves.

"My guess is," Jayden begins, watching me carefully, "that she doesn't want to bring attention to his history. To have to explain how it may have influenced what happened."

"History," I hear myself repeat, wincing at the memory of that word coming out of Ethan's mouth the day he'd said we'd never work.

"With narcotics."

Not real. I feel my stomach drop, the world around me shrinking until it's just me, just Jayden. Just this moment.

As Jayden talks, my stomach keeps dropping and dropping. He tells me about Ethan's arrest junior year for possession, the suspension that followed. Katheryn pulling him out of school, sending him to rehab. How he struggled to stay clean.

Drug use, an arrest record. I've heard rumors of only one other person with a similar history at our high school. It's certainly not something I would have associated with the Ethan I fell for. The version within the fence lines of our bikes, the mural, the orchestra shirts.

Had she known about this, Mom would have waged an all-out war to make sure I did not have any contact with Ethan. Ever.

He was always good at keeping secrets, Bea had told me in the bathroom. *Letting people see just enough to believe what he needed them to believe.*

He intentionally kept this from me. All of it.

Did he think I'd avoid him? Label him? Think less of him? Did he guess how my mom would react?

I wish he had let me in, given me a chance to decide for myself.

20

I RUN. UPHILL. Legs staggering, my breath coming in short, hot gasps. I see him just up ahead. Light brown hair, dark-wash jeans, gray shirt. His bike is on the ground, its front wheel spinning.

He grips the mesh safety fence and starts to climb.

Ethan, no!

I sprint faster. If I can just reach him, pull him back, we can start over and make this right, whatever it takes.

Three yards, two yards, one. I'm diving, throwing myself forward, my arms outstretched.

But the train whistle screams and my hands are empty.

"Nina." Mom's voice at my door.

I turn over and press my face into the pillow. *Not real.*

"It's time to get up."

Not yet. He's just a breath, a step away. If I rewind and try again, this time I'll—

I hear my door swing open, the sharp zip of the blind drawn up. Light intrudes into my room, flagrant and unwelcome. I try to ignore it, get back to the bridge and cover that same ground again, only faster this time.

I have so many questions for him. For this version of Ethan I never got to know.

"We need to talk about booking a venue for your senior

recital," Mom says, her tone businesslike, as if she's at the office and not at home on a Saturday. "Have you looked at the list I sent you? We need to make a decision and put down a deposit as soon as possible."

I slide deeper into my blankets and lie still, hoping she'll leave. My pulse is jumping and my mind feels unsettled, and it isn't just the dream.

Was he using the night he biked to the bridge?

"I noticed you haven't started any of the online modules in the defensive driving course," Mom continues in that same businesslike tone. "Perhaps you can work on that today."

That's not fair! I want to argue. *You never made Carmen do this.*

It's been four weeks since I passed my driver's permit test. I just need practice hours behind the wheel, not a forty-hour online course.

The same weekend Carmen passed her permit test, Dad took her out driving. But he hasn't asked me about going driving, not once.

"Also, we need to go through your closet and look at which clothes to keep or give away. There are just some things you shouldn't be hanging on to, like this . . . strange T-shirt. Where did you get it anyway?"

I jolt upright, pushing the blankets off me. My mirrored closet door stands open, Mom leaning in, tugging at a hanger in the way back.

In a second, I'm across the room, my uncombed hair standing out at odd angles and my pajama top hanging off one shoulder. I snatch the T-shirt out of her hands and slide the closet door shut with a bang.

"Don't *touch* that."

"What's going on here?" Mom snaps.

"This..." I hold up the shirt, my voice shaking, "is mine." I force myself to meet her gaze even though all I want to do is close the blinds and crawl back under the covers.

"You don't wear T-shirts," Mom says, her voice flat. "And I wouldn't start by wearing that one."

"It's..." I look down at the black fabric, smooth a hand over the screen printing. This is the first thing I reach for when I need to feel Ethan here, with me.

Tears spring to my eyes. I feel a sharp ache in my chest and wish for a moment that I could tell her things. Real things like—

I miss him.

And I'm scared.

But instead, I say, "It's a gift."

"Fine." Mom dismisses me with a flick of her wrist. "Get dressed and come downstairs for breakfast. We have a lot to do today."

Right. Her plan for what my day should look like.

Mom's footsteps move down the hall. I fold the T-shirt, place it inside my old violin case, and slide it back on the top shelf in my closet. It should be safe there.

I dress quickly. Pulling on a pair of light-colored jeans and a lavender sweater.

Mom was right, there are a lot of things to do today. The things on her list, but also, something on mine.

21

IT'S 9 P.M. before I finish everything on Mom's list for today.

I'm finally in my room, alone, staring at Katheryn's headshot on the UC Davis faculty website. Gray bob, no makeup, her expression severe and imposing. I search for some resemblance to Ethan, but find none.

It's Doctor, she had corrected me that day we'd first met.

I read now through her impressive list of credentials, publications, and awards in the field of global humanities. Find myself clicking through her publication links, drawn down rabbit holes of ethics, bias, and cultural histories.

I wonder if Ethan had read any of her work. Particularly her article on the impact of emerging technologies on pre-industrial societies around the globe. If he had found himself fascinated, the way I am, by the types of questions she poses, the parallels she draws between completely disparate ideas. All in surprisingly plain language.

It's almost an hour before I remember my purpose, the thing on my to-do list.

Navigating back to the faculty website, I click on the link to Katheryn's UC Davis email just below her headshot.

I had thought I knew what I wanted to say, the questions

I needed to ask. Questions about my version of Ethan and the version I am just now piecing together.

When did he start using?
How long was he in rehab?
Why did he bike to the bridge that night?

But as I type, I can't help feeling there's something more, something bigger behind these questions.

My fingers still on the keyboard as I probe the feeling. It finally comes to me: *Help me understand who Ethan was.*

Could she explain Ethan to me in plain language? At least the parts of him he'd let her see?

Deleting everything, I start over.

Can we meet? I'd really like to talk, I type instead. Then hit send.

Leaning back in my chair, I exhale. It's out, done. The only thing left to do is wait.

My phone buzzes on my desk beside me.

You home?

It's a text from Carmen. The new Carmen I see on social who doesn't text me, call me, or come home. Did something happen to make her reach out?

Yeah, I answer immediately, my body tense.

Can you get the tablet in my room?

I bristle at the request. Really? After months of silence, I'm supposed to be ready to jump and do her bidding? It's like her bossy phase all over again.

You're here? I ask, not quite ready to address her ask. I wish we could talk about Ethan. Talk about my sudden, pressing need to understand him, understand *why*. I wish that she cared.

No. A friend. Outside in the black Nissan.

The brevity of her response stings.

Who is it? I ask, even though I wouldn't know any of her friends now, the ones here or the ones in LA. She doesn't tell me anything, and I miss being a part of her life.

Just give him the tablet.

I suck in a breath, feeling a stab of frustration.

Don't keep him waiting.

I can almost see Carmen pacing, wherever she is. Her lips pinched and brow furrowed, more annoyed with every passing second. I remind myself that I don't have to do this, I can say no. After all, there's string quartet business I need to catch up on, updates to the balance spreadsheet, arrangements that still need to be made for our gigs next Saturday. But instead, I push back from my chair and head down the dark hall to Carmen's room.

Downstairs, my parents are winding down for the night. I hear the drone of the TV in the family room, the clink of a glass on the marble countertop. They're oblivious to Carmen's ask, to the black Nissan outside, to my part in whatever this is.

I stand at Carmen's door like I've done on so many other nights, when I felt like my worries and fears were going to suffocate me. Her bed isn't a bed-boat anymore, that safe space where the gap between us in years, in looks, in worlds seemed to fade. It can't be—not without her inviting me in and asking what's keeping me up, not without her caring.

I hate that, like Ethan, she's also vanished.

Turning the knob, I push open her door and hit the lights.

Books are stacked three deep on her desk, the floor, spilling out beneath her bed. Memoirs, biographies, plays, thrillers, westerns, sci-fi. Carmen devoured it all.

She used to love thrifting for books almost as much as she loved thrifting online for designer brands. Mom hates the idea of secondhand clothes, always buying new for me and Carmen. But to Carmen, you can never have enough clothes, shoes, or books, new or old.

Her collection of tank tops, skirts, jeans, and sweaters are strewn across her bed and lying in heaps on the floor, as if deposited by a tornado. Boots, heels, sneakers, slip-ons perch on top of her dresser and tumble out of her closet.

I sigh. It's definitely as bad as I remember.

Two years ago, my parents had her room repainted and bought her a matching furniture set. They helped her sort through all her stuff, keeping only what she needed and throwing out the rest. A restart of sorts that didn't last. New pen, same pig.

I slog in and work my way from one side of her room to the other, ducking, bending, digging, searching for Carmen's tablet. The whole time, I can feel her—tall, toned frame, flawless skin, designer clothes—staring out at me from the hundreds of photos tacked on the walls. She's everywhere, with everyone, doing everything. Flashing that confident smile, her long black hair falling perfectly in every shot.

I'm rounding the corner of her bed, when my gaze catches on a black-and-white sketch pinned on the wall among all of Carmen's photos. Geometric patterns forming a picture within a picture. I've seen sketches just like this somewhere else, remember studying them in detail—

My gaze dips to the bottom right corner. *E.T.*

Ethan's trademark signature. I'd recognize it anywhere. I just don't understand why it'd be here.

Did Carmen know him? Or did she see this sketch on display somewhere, offer to buy it?

My foot snags an electrical cord. I trip over a space heater and fall hard against her dresser, triggering an avalanche of shoes, old makeup, a box of tampons. My phone buzzes. **Did you find it?**

I want to tell Carmen, *No, sorry.* It's impossible to find anything in this pigsty. But I'm staring at her tablet, brand new and unopened, sitting on top of her dresser. Exposed now by the pile of slop around my feet. Last year's Christmas present from our parents.

Yes, I text back.

I head downstairs, my pace slowing as I near the bottom step. From the family room, I hear the creak of the recliner, the drone of the news channel on TV. Dad won't go upstairs for another hour, but Mom—

Her firm footsteps come suddenly down the hall.

I shrink back against the wall and try to do something with the tablet box. I hide it behind my back, then tuck it under my sweater. Already I can hear her questions—

"Mel?" Dad calls.

Mom sighs, the sound just on the other side of the wall. Too close for comfort.

"What is it?" Her voice fades with her footsteps, back down the hall and into the family room.

Releasing my breath, I bolt out the front door and down the driveway, silent in my bare feet. The black Nissan idles at the curb, headlights off.

As I head toward the car, the passenger side window lowers with a smooth hum. The driver is Carmen's age, maybe a year older, with steel-gray eyes, brown hair, and a stocky build.

"That's it?" He snatches the boxed tablet. "She didn't give you anything else?"

I don't like the way he's looking at me, his gray eyes sliding from my face to my chest. I hate the method with which he fingers the box, looking for dents and scratches, like he's done this a hundred times before.

I want to snatch it away. It's a gift from my parents to Carmen, a tool for her to use in college. But instead, I take a step back, my mind still spinning.

22

IT'S SUNDAY NIGHT and my phone is blowing up with messages in the youth group chat.

The one I've been meaning to turn off notifications for.

EPIC WEEKEND!!!!

Roger's message to the group followed by photos of the sledding trip and the potluck.

Way too many pictures of a poorly-built snowman. Lucy on a plastic disc flying down the hill, hair crazy and face twisted in a grimace. A side of her I've never seen. Roger posing next to a crackling fire in Traci's backyard. Both his eyebrows intact this time.

I feel a twinge of sadness scrolling through these photos. Like I should have been there. Helping to build a *proper* snowman, roasting marshmallows in Roger's first successful fire (so proud, so proud!).

Instead, my weekend has been anything but epic.

After delivering the tablet last night, I went back to Carmen's room to take a closer look at the sketch on her wall.

The geometric patterns, the picture within a picture. It was definitely Ethan's work. I unpinned it carefully from the wall, checking to see if there was an inscription on the back. Some kind of clue to let me know how, exactly, she got this.

But the back of the sketch was blank.

Carmen was always good at striking up conversations with perfect strangers, drawing out their interests, their passions in a matter of minutes. Maybe she'd met Ethan that way. Asked to see his art.

The messages in the group chat are slowing down now. I set my phone aside, glancing at Ethan's sketch that now sits on my desk, protected in a clear-view folder.

I wish I could check my phone and find a new message from him. Something more than—

See you tomorrow, then?
Yeah.

My text to Ethan at ten the night he biked to the bridge. His text back to me at 10:40.

Somehow, I still can't bring myself to believe that's it. That's all there ever will be.

My memories are choppy following Ethan's last three words to me by the literature building in December: *You. Me. This.*

I remember passing the mural after school, hoping to find him up on a ladder, a paint palette in one hand and a brush in the other. His favorite granola bar tucked into the pocket of his jeans. But he was never there.

I stared at his photo in the school paper. The one of him leaning back against the mural, gazing off into the distance. Wondering why he agreed to let the article run before completing all his finishing touches.

There was a familiar tension at home in the weeks leading up to Christmas. Dad and Rich working around the clock to try to fix things with the startup.

On Christmas day, we arrived at Uncle Edward's without

Carmen. Mom attempting to excuse her with the same story she used for Thanksgiving. Citing Carmen's demanding double major, her need to focus. It didn't go over well.

We left early that night because I had a 7 A.M. flight to Denver the next morning for YMI. Another thing that didn't go over well.

New state, new city, new people. Eating, sleeping, and playing my violin with some of the best teen musicians in the United States. The dream I'd worked so hard for. Yet boarding the plane, all I felt was hollow.

It wasn't until I was in my dorm room, meeting my YMI roommate—cellist by day, gamer by night, Julia Kranston—that I finally got the text.

Hey.

Ethan's name in bold on my message app. I sucked in a breath, almost dizzy from the sudden surge of emotions. Elation, hope, anger, pain—

For the first time in weeks, I felt alive.

Can I see you?

The split was so sudden, so unexpected. Followed by weeks of complete silence, of hating that I missed him, of feeling lost, empty without him. Now, just as abruptly, he was back. I didn't know what to think.

At YMI, I typed back, deciding to keep my response short, simple.

Oh, right.

In my head, I could almost see him shrug, as if YMI, the major experience he knew I'd been anticipating and the reason he'd stopped talking to me, had slipped his mind. I'd felt a familiar bitterness in my throat thinking of the times he mentioned seeing Bea's band play. But he'd never made it to any of my violin or orchestra performances.

Maybe you can let me know, he messaged, **how things go there.**

I bit my lip, all too aware that if I did reply, I'd be back in this—

"Who are you talking to?" Julia asked, leaning over my shoulder. I'd just met her a half hour ago and already, she was in my space.

"No one," I answered.

Hot Cheeto breath assaulted me as Julia pushed in closer, squinting at his thumbnail photo on my app. Her hands swooped down, seizing my phone.

"Hey!"

"Damn," she mused, lips pursed, broad shoulders hunched. Her cheese-stained fingers squeaked across my spotless screen to zoom. "He's cute."

"Aren't you in the middle of a quest or whatever?" I snapped, grappling for my phone.

"Laptop crashed. It's rebooting now."

Julia wandered back to her desk and dropped heavily into her swivel chair, keeping it turned in my direction.

"So, what's the deal with this guy?" Her small green eyes probed me as I bent over my phone, carefully cleaning its surface with a disinfectant wipe.

"It's . . ." I glanced down at his thumbnail photo. One I'd taken of him at the awards dinner we'd attended together at the university. "Complicated," I finally admitted, knowing already that I'd reply to Ethan. Get back in this . . . whatever it was.

I pick up my phone again now and stare at the message string with Ethan that's so far down I have to scroll to find it. It moves farther down each day, each week that passes. I have to do something to bring it back to the top—

Can I see you? I type, then hit send.

The same message he sent that had brought us back together again.

My heart beats thick in my chest. There's no reason to hope, but I still—

A response pops up. **Message not delivered.**

23

"NINA," ROGER URGES as he pulls out of the school parking lot and onto the road. "You have *got* to try some of these."

I glance at the Costco-sized bag of chips sitting on the console between us.

"They're multigrain." Roger pops in another mouthful and crunches loudly. "With *flaxseed*." He raises his brows at me like that last little detail should change my mind.

"I'm not hungry," I say, checking my email app for the tenth time today. It's Tuesday, and Katheryn Travvers has yet to respond to my message from Saturday night asking if we could meet.

"Not hungry?" Roger exclaims. "For snacks? Come on, Nina. You used to come to youth group just for the junk food."

"True." I reach in the bag for a chip, then another. My eyes roll back as I stifle a groan. *So* good. "But these don't really count as junk food," I note. "Considering all the health benefits."

"The best of both worlds," Roger says with a smile.

I ponder that phrase as he makes the turn onto the bridge over the tracks.

When I first met Ethan, all I could see was his talent and creativity, his limitless potential. I thought we'd complement each other. Ethan supporting my music while I supported his art, inspiring the best versions of ourselves.

The best of both our worlds.

But somehow that only worked one way. While I gave up my time, my attention, to support his art, he never attended my orchestra concerts or hung out during my quartet practices. When he mentioned an interest in art school, I encouraged him to put together a portfolio. But when I talked about YMI or the music colleges I was applying to, he seemed almost resentful.

Maybe that was what he meant when he said we'd "never work."

I wince. The memory of those words still hits me hard, like a punch in the gut.

I wonder now, what led him to reach out when I was at YMI. Why break the silence? Were things complicated with that *someone else* Bea had suggested that day in the bathroom? Was he struggling with the addictions he'd hidden so carefully from me? Or did he simply miss me?

I was tired of not having answers.

"Turn right here," I say suddenly as we approach the intersection where we would usually make a left to get to my house.

Roger glances at me, his brow furrowed. "What's to the right?" he asks, his voice muffled with the crunching of chips.

"I'd ... like to see if someone's home."

"Who?" Roger asks, flipping his turn signal and making two terrifying lane changes.

"Dr. Travvers, if you must know," I admit, watching him carefully.

Roger only nods. "Ethan's mom."

"Right." I let out a breath. It's almost a relief to hear someone else say Ethan's name.

"So, what am I looking for here?" Roger asks, glancing along the tree-lined street we turned onto. "A house number?"

"It's the duplex community on the left, just up ahead." I feel my pulse start to pound as we approach. I want nothing more than to sit down with Ethan's mom and just talk. But now that we're in his neighborhood, I'm worried about how she'll receive me, scared of what she will have to say.

Roger turns in, circling the court. "Park anywhere?"

"Yeah." I grab my backpack and hop out as soon as he puts Annabel in park. "I'll be right back."

"Do you want me to go with you?" Roger asks, concern in his dark brown eyes.

I hesitate for just a second, my hand still on the passenger side door. "I'll be fine," I say, turning to head up the front walk. But there's a small catch in my voice.

My steps are heavy with the weight of memories as I approach the door. I can almost see Ethan and I swinging off our bikes and pushing them up the walk that day he gave me the shirt.

I knock, a lump rising in my throat as I notice the water spigot we had chained our bikes to. There's a small leak, the water slowly beading up and then dropping to the ground with a splat.

There are no footsteps coming toward the door. No sounds at all, except for my shallow breaths.

I glance back at the street to find Roger standing outside

his car, arms folded, watching me. Like a very tall, very skinny bodyguard.

I try again, ringing the doorbell this time. The sudden, grating buzz almost makes me jump.

No answer.

I ring it one more time before finally giving up.

"No luck?" Roger asks as I approach his car.

I shake my head. I was in such a hurry to get to the front door I didn't even look at the cars on the street. Didn't notice the absence of Katheryn's old Corolla. The one with the yellow bumper sticker Ethan hated still firmly attached. The sticker commemorating the year before they moved to Davis, the last year Ethan ever made honor roll.

"Thanks," I say, turning to Roger as we leave the duplex community. "For taking me."

"Anytime." Roger flashes me another big smile.

I stare down at my hands clasped tightly in my lap. I feel a pressure behind my eyes and in my chest.

"I'm here, you know," Roger offers. "If you need to talk."

I nod, keeping my eyes on my clasped hands. Afraid that if I speak, start telling him about all the memories that keep surfacing, the jarring truths I've learned, the pain I feel—I won't be able to stop, won't be able to control the flood. All my deepest emotions and thoughts brought out into the open. Raw and messy and broken. What will he think of me then?

It's better to keep it all inside, I remind myself.

"All right, Nina," Roger says, breaking the silence as he pulls up to the curb in front of my house. "Here we are!"

He says this as if it should be accompanied by the blowing of trumpets. If excitement is contagious, I must be immune to Roger's.

I raise a hand in a wave as he pulls away and head quickly up the driveway, digging into my backpack for my house keys. But before I can get my key in the lock, someone pulls the front door open.

I freeze on the doormat, staring.

"Carmen!"

"Nina." Carmen raises her brows, as if amused at my reaction.

Her bleached blond hair is chopped up to the neck, the edges ragged. A cheap oversized cotton T-shirt and gray sweatpants hang off her tall frame. The kind of clothes Mom would never approve of. She's gained weight, around her waist, her thighs. Her skin, always sickeningly perfect, is blotchy, some areas dark with scars.

She's Carmen, but not Carmen.

"When did you get back?" I hear the tightness in my voice. It's hard to believe she's here, right in front of me.

"A couple hours ago."

"Who picked you up?"

"Danny." She shrugs. "You don't know him."

Of course I don't. I hate the way her words make me feel, as if she's doing me a favor just by speaking to me when we used to tell each other everything.

"Anyways"—she steps back from the door as I step in—"I shouldn't have let Danny leave without getting me a coffee first. There's nothing in this house, Nina. No snacks, no soda, no nothing."

She says this as if she's never lived here before.

"How long are you here for?" I ask, shutting the front door behind me.

"Oh," she says lightly, "I'm just ... passing through."

I watch as she shambles down the hall, reaching around to pull up the waistband of her sweats.

Something in her voice makes me question if she's telling the truth.

24

VOICES ARGUE DOWNSTAIRS.

Mom, exclaiming over Carmen's hair, her skin, her clothes. Carmen shouting that it's her hair, her body, and she's sick of trying to measure up.

The garage door rumbles open and then shuts. Dad's home. He asks Carmen what she's doing here in the middle of the week, partway through winter quarter. I lean over the upstairs banister to hear better.

"I thought you wanted me to come back!"

"Yes, during your school breaks." Dad's voice sounds tired, and I'm surprised he's not immediately taking her side. "But not at this critical juncture when you should be studying, working to improve your GPA."

"Fine," Carmen threatens. "I'll leave then."

An explosion of voices.

Mom exclaiming, "You just got here!" Her voice hungry, almost desperate.

Dad insisting, "Nobody's asking you to leave."

Both of them trying to get her to stay.

Carmen's footsteps come up the stairs and I quickly slip back down the hall and to my room.

I hear her door open and shut. She's on the phone now, talking, laughing, like everything is fine, just fine. Like she didn't just drop in on her family unannounced after months of evasion. Like she's not a totally different person.

I stare at the notifications on my phone. A new message from Lucy asking for an extra practice session for the string quartet to prep for the two events on Saturday. A reminder from my calendar app to complete my music scholarship applications, study for my government test.

I hear the clatter of pans on the stove, the low rumble of my parents' voices in the kitchen. The aroma of sizzling meat and vegetables drifts up the stairs—Mom preparing another home-cooked, Chinese-style dinner.

I open my calendar app, searching for another late afternoon or evening slot that would work for everyone in the string quartet. But it's hard to think, hard to plan, when all I hear is Carmen's phone conversation down the hall, droning on and on and on.

I want to rap on her door and have her invite me in, have a conversation with *me*. It's been such a long time since we talked, really talked. I want to tell her about everything that happened since last October, ask her about Ethan's sketch—the one I took from her room. How did she get it? Does she know that he's gone?

"Dinner!" Mom calls.

I put down my phone and head for the stairs. Mom expects everyone to assemble as soon as dinner is announced.

As I pass Carmen's room, I hear her ask, "Are you outside? I'll be right there."

Who's outside? Is it Danny who dropped her off? Or someone else I don't know? Surely she remembers Mom's Basic Rule about showing up for dinner.

Carmen's door swings open. She's wearing a faded black

zip-up hoodie over her cheap cotton shirt. It seems too light, too flimsy for the chilly night air.

"You're not eating?" I ask, as she follows me down the stairs.

"No," she snaps, like sitting down to Mom's home-cooked meal is the last thing she wants to do. "I need a pizza."

She heads for the front door, shoving her socked feet into a pair of slides on her way out.

"Carmen!" Mom calls, hurrying down the hall from the kitchen, a wooden spatula still in one hand. She yanks open the front door and leans out. "Carmen!"

But there is no answer except for the sound of a car driving away, fast.

"Who picked her up?" Mom asks, turning to me as she shuts the door. "Did she tell you?"

"No." I follow her into the kitchen. "She didn't say."

Beside the dining room table, Dad paces with his phone pressed to his ear. "A leak, right," he says to whoever is on the other end. "In the accounting books. That's what the third-party audit team told me."

He rubs a hand over his face. He looks beat-down, tired. All the round-the-clock work hours since December, trying to right things at the startup, seem to be catching up to him. "They found unapproved travel expenses: airfare, hotels, meals. No supporting documentation for the trips."

"Vin." Mom gestures for him to wrap up the call.

Dad nods. "Sure. Let me know what you find."

"Was that Rich?" Mom asks as soon as Dad gets off the phone.

"It's Philip," Dad says, taking his seat at the table. "From research and development. He's helping me with the strategy for the restructuring. Rich has been . . . unavailable."

"Unavailable?" Mom frowns. "But he's your *Chief Operating Officer.*"

"Things are messy for him right now with the divorce." Dad's gaze darts quickly in my direction as if reminding Mom that I'm sitting right here.

Not that it matters. I've already heard about Rich's alleged affair, his sports gambling, his wife filing for divorce.

Mom nods, dropping the subject. She picks up her chopsticks only to set them down again.

I know she's thinking about Carmen. We all are.

"I'll look into it," Dad says, reaching suddenly across the table, his hand brushing hers. "Call the school."

Mom doesn't say anything, but she doesn't move her hand either.

After dinner, I set up my music stand beside the piano and switch on the floor lamp. I practice the last section of the first movement of the Bartók concerto. I know I should be studying for my government test, working on my music scholarship applications. But I ache to feel the music, its sweetness and power.

Instead, the music stays one-dimensional, a finger-crippling piece that doesn't fill the hollowness inside.

When I head upstairs to get ready for bed, I see Carmen's toiletries scattered across the counter of the bathroom we used to share. Retainer, mouthwash, contact lens solution, mascara.

My throat tightens at the sight of her things. I remember all the times I stood at her door, my fingers resting lightly on her doorknob, touching but not turning. Letting myself imagine for a moment what it would be like to step in and find my sister there.

She's home, but it's nothing like what I pictured it would be.

In the morning, the light outside is gray, and through my window I see rain falling in sheets. Carmen isn't in her room and her toiletries on the bathroom counter are untouched.

I hear my parents talking in the kitchen. As I get dressed and head downstairs, I feel a tugging at the back of my mind, as if I'm forgetting something about today. Something important.

"*What?*" Mom's voice explodes as I reach the bottom of the stairs. "How long has she known about this? Was she hoping we wouldn't find out?"

I hang back in the hall, listening.

"She probably didn't want to acknowledge what was happening." I can just see Dad leaning against the kitchen island in his suit and tie, nursing a cup of coffee. "Like it would just somehow go away."

"But she took summer session," Mom sputters. "It should have helped."

"It wasn't enough, Mel."

"Nina." Mom's voice is strained as I walk in. She smooths a hand over her flat-ironed hair, blinking quickly. "There's fruit salad in the fridge. Cottage cheese."

I nod, grabbing a bowl from the cupboard and a spoon from the drawer. Pretend I don't notice Mom dab at her eyes. She's not one to cry.

A key turns in the front door lock.

"Carmen!" Mom disappears from the kitchen, Dad just a step behind. Setting my bowl down on the counter, I follow.

"Where did you go last night? Who were you with? How could you just—"

"I don't have time for this." Carmen's voice is high-pitched, feverish. She's in the same clothes as yesterday but now they stink of smoke. "I need to go. I'm barely going to make it back for afternoon classes as it is."

"You 'need to go'?" Mom repeats slowly. "Where?"

"*School. Class.*" Carmen lunges for the stairs, her short bleached hair mussed and wet with rain.

"There's no need to lie to us, Carmen." Dad steps in front of her, his jaw tight, gaze pained.

"I don't know what you're talking about," Carmen counters. But her voice catches, her words tripping one over the other.

"I think," Dad says slowly, "you do."

"I don't see what—" Carmen begins forcefully. "It's not like—"

The words rush out only to vaporize, leaving her with nothing.

"Why didn't you tell us you were dismissed?" Dad presses.

Dismissed. Done.

The room seems to spin, the floor tilting beneath my feet. This time it's not just academic probation, a lost volleyball scholarship. Carmen's finally out. Out of chances, out of time.

Not real.

The very air seems to have been sucked out of the room as I wait along with my parents for her to come clean, explain herself.

"The school gave you chance after chance!" Mom's harsh tone splits the silence. I flinch on Carmen's behalf, thinking of the tone Mom used with me—hard and accusing—the day she picked me up from the bridge after Ethan jumped. "*We* gave you chance after chance," Mom continues. "Everything you needed to succeed and you just threw it—"

"Shut up!" Carmen's chin trembles, a sob bursting from her chest. "Just *shut up!*"

"Carmen—" Dad reaches for her shoulder, but she dodges past, pounding up the stairs to her room.

Her door slams. We hear her crying, beating her fists against the wall, her wails raw and pathetic.

A car horn beeps in the driveway. Two short blasts, waking me as if from a dream.

25

NOT REAL, I tell myself. *Not real.*

I head to fourth period government, Carmen's sobs still ringing in my head.

It isn't until Mr. Apte is passing out the test that I realize I didn't study last night. I swallow, my head spinning as my stomach twists.

Was this the tugging reminder I'd felt earlier?

I stare down at the full page of multiple choice and fill-ins. Basic questions straight out of the government textbook. Had I read the chapters last night, I would know this.

My knee bounces, my fingertips tapping soundlessly on my desk. Staring, staring at the questions, hoping something comes to me. All around me, heads are bent, pencils scratching against paper. Everyone focused, prepared.

"One minute!"

Drawing in a tight breath, I reread the questions, but nothing computes. Just like all the other questions I grapple with, like why someone like Carmen could get dismissed from college. Or why Ethan Travvers is dead at seventeen.

"That's time."

I look up to find the classroom almost empty. Jumping to my feet, I scramble to collect my things and follow the last few stragglers to the front of the room.

"How are you doing, Nina?" Mr. Apte asks as I drop my half-finished test on his desk, face down. There is sympathy in his gaze and I wonder if this is all part of the postvention protocols, the tools rolled out at the mandatory assembly.

"Fine." I try to force a smile, but fall short.

"Anything new?" he asks.

"My sister's home." The words pop out, unexpectedly.

"Carmen!" Mr. Apte lights up. "She's in her sophomore year at UCLA, right?"

I shouldn't have brought her up. Especially to Mr. Apte, who is the staff advisor for Honor Society and Model United Nations, two clubs Carmen had leadership positions in all through high school.

"Yes." Except she's not enrolled. At least not anymore.

"A major in microbiology and a minor in entrepreneurship." Mr. Apte shakes his head. "It's a lot to take on. But then again, it's Carmen."

"Right." I edge backward, needing an exit from this conversation.

Carmen's old friends, teachers, coaches—they only remember one version of her, the overachiever who was voted Most Likely to Succeed. It's best to keep it that way.

AFTER SCHOOL, LUCY and I wait at the curb of the parking lot for her mom to pick us up. We're heading to Peter Kapoor's house for quartet practice, the first of two practice sessions this week. I still can't seem to shake the feeling from this morning, like I'm forgetting something important.

"I know it's back-to-back practices, but I'm glad tomorrow night ended up working out for everyone," Lucy says.

I nod, but my mind is still on the government test, my

stomach tightening at the thought of a failing grade. How could I possibly explain that to Mom?

"What do you think about focusing on the anniversary party playlist this afternoon?" Lucy asks. "There's a couple of new arrangements in that set."

"Sure," I say, my response automatic. I haven't practiced any of the pieces for the gigs this coming Saturday, but Lucy doesn't need to know that.

"Hello, hello!" Lucy's mom, Brenda, pulls up to the curb in an older silver Subaru. "How nice to see *you*, Nina. It's been a while."

"Hi, Mrs. Beyers," I say, sliding into the back seat and setting my violin case down beside me. "Thanks for giving us a ride."

"Of course, of course." Mrs. Beyers waves away the thanks. She has the same red hair as Lucy and her perm is about as big and bold as I remember. "Lucy says you attended YMI. What an *achievement*. Did you know Lucy's embroidery has just *taken off*? She was a guest speaker at the embroidery conference in Texas. If it weren't for that, you two could have been roommates at the music camp."

"Intensive," Lucy corrects, but Mrs. Beyers also waves that away.

"Princeton is Lucy's number one school. Did she tell you that?" Mrs. Beyers continues. "*I* think she has a good chance, with all her extracurriculars, her high SAT scores, and all those AP classes."

I hold back a groan. Every time Mom, Mrs. Kishimoto, and Mrs. Beyers get together for the occasional lunch, Mom comes home with glowing accolades about Lucy and with areas of improvement for me.

"I'm sure she's a strong candidate," I offer.

"She certainly is," Mrs. Beyers affirms. "What's your number one school, Nina? Lucy mentions you're interested in a conservatory?"

"Three actually—"

"That's just wonderful," Mrs. Beyers bubbles. "Lucy would have applied to a conservatory, but she's interested in studying mechanical engineering. Of course, with a major like that, there's not much time for music. Well, what do you know? Here we are at Peter's. Have a good time, okay?"

I breathe a sigh of relief as Mrs. Beyers drives away.

"Sorry about that," Lucy says, as we walk through a swinging iron gate and up to Peter's door. "She likes to talk."

I shrug. "It's fine. Really." But hearing that note of pride in Mrs. Beyers' voice as she listed off Lucy's various accomplishments, reminded me of Grandma. The way her chest seemed to puff out whenever she recounted Carmen's achievements. Putting her up on a pedestal.

I draw in a sharp breath, wondering how much longer Mom can hide the truth about my sister.

"So, what are we working on first?" Madison asks, as we sit on folding chairs in Peter's crowded living room.

I hear the sizzle of oil from the kitchen. Peter's mom and aunts talking and laughing, frying up batches of something. The air smells both spicy and syrupy.

"I've got an agenda for today and tomorrow," Lucy announces, pulling out a folder and distributing a neatly typed list. "We'll focus on the anniversary playlist today and during the first part of our practice session tomorrow night. The wedding playlist is pretty much there. But I've added a couple pieces we could polish during the second half of our practice session tomorrow."

Why did she ask me about focusing on the anniversary playlist today, if she already had it in print?

"Wow," Peter exclaims. "So organized!"

I blink down at the agenda, feeling blindsided. Lucy may be concertmistress in symphony orchestra, but *I* run this string quartet—not her.

"Before we start with the first piece," Lucy continues, "I was thinking we could warm up with some scales."

"We always do that," Madison says, pushing some straggling curls back from her face.

"Yes." Lucy clears her throat daintily. "On our own. But this time, maybe we could try it together."

In my head, I see us back in the library that day I first met Ethan. Lucy taking over the design for the shirts without ever consulting me.

"When did you decide all this?" I ask, trying to keep my voice low, calm.

Lucy straightens in her chair. Today, her hand-embroidered sweater says, CHANGE IS GOOD. I wonder if she wore it on purpose. "I'm just trying to help, Nina. Make sure we're prepared for Saturday, that's all."

I don't believe her. She's trying to edge me out, take over. I want to call her out on it, but I feel Madison and Peter's gazes on us, the question marks in their eyes.

"Sure," I say, instead, with a light shrug. Even though I feel heat rising up my neck, the sting of tears in my eyes. "Let's start with scales."

From scales we move to the pieces listed on Lucy's agenda.

I'm sight-reading most of the music, whole sections I haven't practiced. Trying to keep up, but knowing I'm skipping notes and my timing is off.

It's a relief when we break for the day, Peter disappearing into the kitchen and returning with a heaping plate of Indian snacks—a mix of sweet and spicy.

I help myself to a handful of the spicy snacks. Mom never makes anything deep fried, which is a shame since it tastes so good.

"Tomorrow," Lucy says, as she nibbles on a sweet snack, going all around the edges before eating the center. "Let's be prepared to run through those same pieces during the first hour."

I feel her blue gaze slide toward me, as if her message carried special significance.

But I stare straight ahead, crunching on my snacks.

These events we play at—graduation parties, anniversaries, weddings—they're milestones celebrating life. Days passing, years passing, rites of passage coming and going. I take it all for granted.

That tugging in the back of my mind. The feeling that there was something important . . .

I swallow hard as a familiar pain grips my chest.

Eighteen. Ethan would have turned eighteen today. A milestone. Something we could have celebrated together. Except he's gone.

26

FRIDAY MORNING, DAD takes an early flight to LA, extricating himself from the company restructuring to fly down, pack up Carmen's things, and drive her car home. All the pieces that must be cleaned up in the wake of Carmen's dismissal.

He isn't back by dinner and we eat without him, Carmen picking at Mom's oven-baked char siu drumsticks with about as much enthusiasm as she had for getting her wisdom teeth pulled last year.

My music stand is set up by the piano, the sheet music for the string quartet already laid out. I should really practice tonight, get everything polished for the events tomorrow. But I walk right past my music stand and head upstairs to my room.

Ethan's sketch is still on my desk and for a second, I think about taking it to Carmen's room and asking her about it. But she doesn't seem to miss it. So, instead, I sit on my bed, flipping through photos on my phone from Katheryn's faculty award dinner last November.

Ethan in gray slacks and a black tie. Me in a blue dress and black flats.

There are plates of sliced roast and mashed potatoes in front of us. Ice water in wine glasses.

Instead of my usual low ponytail, I'd worn my hair down and applied some eye shadow and mascara. I zoom in to one of the pictures, staring at our faces. We looked *good* together.

I had walked into the venue with Ethan, wondering if I'd made the right choice in coming, my head spinning with all the things I still needed to do.

As we took our seats at Katheryn's table, Ethan had caught my eye. *Thank you*, he'd mouthed, and just like that, the spinning thoughts in my head silenced.

Other things come back to me now, little things. Ethan's touch on the small of my back as he leaned in to whisper "Bor-ing" during the speeches. The clink of our wine glasses as we toasted each other with our ice waters. Ethan retrieving my napkin from under the table when it slipped off my lap.

Sitting side by side all evening, our shoulders almost, but not quite, touching. I'd felt that same pull from that day in his room when he gave me the shirt. Wondered if he too wished we could pick up where we had left off then. But Katheryn had watched us closely all night, her eyes narrowed, lips pressed in a thin line.

It wasn't until we were walking across the heavily treed parking lot to Katheryn's car, that Ethan pulled me back into the shadows. Our hands twining as he leaned down and I tilted my head up. Our lips meeting in a perfect kiss.

Warmth floods my veins at the memory. I wish I could go back to that very moment when everything felt *right* between us.

Drawing a steadying breath, I flip through the rest of the selfies that Ethan and I took.

Pensive. Giddy. Sophisticated. Clueless. Our expressions

mutate from one shot to the next. Thirty seconds of takes—some on point, others not so much. Just something to do before the presentation of awards. Never meant to be a collection of "lasts," cataloged, scrutinized, and grieved over.

A thickness rises in my throat. My fingers clench, knuckles whitening.

More.

There was supposed to be more. More moments. More life. More everything—

I hear the rumble of the garage door opening, Dad coming home.

Moving from my bed to the window, I peer out just in time to see the taillights of Carmen's car flash once before the garage door slides smoothly shut.

I stay at the window even after I hear Dad come in through the garage door. I look out at the large homes, the elaborate yards, the empty street. Picture-perfect on the outside.

A weight settles over me, rooting me in place. Carmen's car in the garage, her things packed inside. I didn't realize until now that I'd been holding on to hope that it was all a mistake. That any day, Carmen would be heading back to LA to finish her sophomore year. Work her way back into good academic standing and to her place on Grandma's pedestal.

But instead, she's dismissed, here to stay. Losing everything I've seen her work so hard for.

Nothing is as it should be with Carmen back and Ethan gone.

THE NEXT DAY, I'm dragging hard. There's a persistent heaviness in my head and limbs that makes me want to crawl back into bed. But I force myself to get dressed in a white blouse, black cardigan, and long black skirt.

I used to love the marathon days of back-to-back gigs. The preparation, the flurry of activity, an excuse to drink copious amounts of coffee to keep up with it all.

But even with coffee, I'm dreading today.

Lucy and Madison are already in Peter's driveway when Mom drops me off at ten-thirty in the morning. We pack our supplies and equipment into the back of Peter's station wagon. Then drive fifty minutes to Napa, making a pit stop at an In-N-Out to get burgers before heading to the wedding venue.

We pull up to an estate with a stunning view of the hills. Hand-lettered signs direct us to the back of the property.

A wide brick courtyard, paper lanterns hanging from trees, white plastic chairs set up in rows on either side of the aisle. It's all I have time to take in before the wedding planner ushers us to the far-left corner of the courtyard.

"You can set up here. Remember to look for my cue on when to switch to the processional music."

Quickly, I review our pieces in the few minutes we have after setting up, trying to focus on any potential trouble spots.

"You look tired, Nina." Lucy's gaze sweeps over me as we warm up with scales—her idea. "Did you get enough sleep?"

"Yes," I answer, even though I didn't.

We launch into our playlist as the guests arrive and take their places. Classy background music to set the atmosphere.

A throbbing starts in my temples as the wedding program begins and we switch to the processional. I probably shouldn't have had the Double-Double burger . . .

I fight through the headache, hitting all the right notes at the right times—but just barely, focusing like my life depends on it.

My brain feels shot by the time we arrive at the anniversary party five hours later. The party was supposed to be outside in the couple's backyard on their bluestone patio. But they moved it last minute to a ballroom on the university campus, citing rain in the forecast.

It isn't until we're walking through the door of the ballroom that I recognize the space.

The patterned carpet, the circular tables, the large projector screen mounted at the front of the room. The tablecloths are white and gold instead of blue and white, but it all looks the same, feels the same as when Ethan and I walked in here.

Something squeezes hard in my chest.

I feel an unsteadiness in my hands as we get set up. The feeling intensifies when we start to play.

Two tables away, Ethan had pulled out a chair for me, caught my eye and mouthed *thank you*, as we sat down.

I bite my lip, try to steady my hand on the bow. Perhaps I did only know him in part. Had seen only the parts of him he wanted me to see. But I still miss him.

I miss him so, so much.

It's been a week now since I sent my email to Katheryn with no response. Perhaps my request to meet was too much to ask, too soon. But if so, couldn't she just tell me that? Or is the problem not meeting up, but meeting up with *me*?

Something strikes my ankle. Hard.

I tuck my foot beneath my folding chair, but whatever it is, kicks again.

"You're playing my part!" Lucy hisses.

I turn to find her staring at me, her brow furrowed and lips turned down. Beside her, Peter and Madison exchange a pointed look.

My breath catches as I glance at the sheet music. I really messed up.

"Lovely music." A large-boned woman with a cleft chin stands in front of us, a glass of wine in her hand. She's looking at me and I squirm, wondering if she picked up on my earlier mistake.

"Thank you," Lucy offers when I don't respond. "I know you had to pivot last minute, but this place looks great. Love the decorations."

The lady grimaces. "It was definitely a scramble, moving everything here. But now it can rain all night if it wants to."

Lucy, Madison, and Peter laugh appreciatively.

"Anyways, we're starting the video we made for my parents in a few minutes. Feel free to refresh yourselves. There's plenty of food." The lady gestures at the lavish charcuterie spread behind her.

Video for her parents . . .

Like gears turning in molasses, I feel the pieces slowly click into place. This is Ann, the lady who booked us. We'd met with her last month to go over all the details.

"Will do. Thank you, Ann." Lucy flashes her gracious, endearing smile, the kind of smile that secures a return customer.

That smile fades when Lucy looks at me. "What's going on, Nina?"

I flinch at the accusation in her tone. "Nothing. I've just been . . ." *Tired. Distracted. Sad.*

"I know things have been tough," Lucy says, her voice low. "But we're a business and people pay for us to come prepared. You seem like . . . you don't even want to be here."

"I do," I snap, setting my violin down and thumping the case shut. "It's just a bad week."

Lucy purses her lips. "Mr. Martinez and I have been talking and we think you need some time off, Nina. Starting tomorrow."

My body stiffens, my senses alert. "What are you saying?"

"I'm saying," Lucy hazards, as if already bracing for my rebuttal, "that maybe—"

"*Seriously.*" Peter comes up behind us with a loaded plate of cured meat, cheese, and pickles. "Why aren't you guys eating? The spread is great!"

"Oooh, is that Manchego?" Madison asks, helping herself to a piece of cheese from his plate.

"Hey!" Peter exclaims, flicking away her hand. "Get your own."

"I was saying," Lucy turns back to me, ignoring the interruption, "maybe you're not in the right place to run the quartet."

"I didn't know there was a 'right place.'" I bite off each word like it's my last. Madison and Peter step in closer, looking between us, their brows raised.

"We're . . . concerned." Lucy fiddles with the scalloped collar of her black dress. I see Madison and Peter nodding behind her in agreement. "If you need time off, we can handle things."

"*I* never said anything about time off," I counter, hating the lump that just keeps growing in my throat. "*You're* the one kicking me out."

"No one's kicking you out," Lucy insists. "We care about you—"

"Just stop talking. *Please.*" Turning on my heel, I walk out of the ballroom, my long black skirt swishing as I try to distance myself from the memories.

27

"WHAT DO YOU mean you're 'taking a break' from the string quartet?" Mom demands as we work together in the backyard, Mom pruning her prize garden roses as I clean out the dead leaves and scrub the stains from the supposedly "low-maintenance" water feature.

The results for the government test came back Tuesday. When Mom found out I scored 62 percent, I immediately lost phone privileges for the week and was assigned dirty-labor jobs through the weekend.

As I scoop the slimy leaves into a bucket, I can't help but wonder why Carmen isn't also out here, why she still gets to keep her phone. It doesn't seem fair, especially since she hasn't followed up on the community college applications and volunteer opportunities Mom keeps reminding her about.

"It means I won't be involved going forward." I feel my stomach twist, remembering the meeting with Mr. Martinez on Monday. When he confirmed that Lucy was officially going to take over as lead and that they'd find a sub for me while I "took a break."

The whole drive home, Roger tried to pry out what was wrong, a concerned furrow between his brows. I wanted to spill my guts. Tell him it was his girlfriend who edged me out. Lay out *my* side of the story for him to judge. But the thought of it getting back to Lucy kept me from sharing.

"And why not?" Mom presses, reaching up to readjust her large, wide-brimmed hat. "Your lead role on the string quartet is part of your college applications."

"I guess I wasn't performing . . . as well as I should?" The statement comes out as more of a question, yet it still hurts to admit.

"Then you need to try harder," Mom says. Like it's just that simple. "There's still your senior recital—make *sure* it's perfect."

For the next two and a half weeks, I try to find my way back to my world before Ethan, with all its structure, rules, and ruthless predictability.

I study in the library after school, practice my Bartók concerto in the evenings. With great difficulty, I push through the first movement of the concerto and into the second. I feel the pressure mounting, time slipping away before my senior recital. It's already February, a short month, with my senior recital just around the corner in April.

Without the lead role for the string quartet, I have no excuses. Nothing to stop me from learning the piece and playing it well enough for Grandma to finally notice me, too.

Every year, Grandma hosts a party at her sprawling mansion just south of San Francisco. A celebration of her birthday, which, depending on the year, falls around Chinese New Year. Aunts, uncles, cousins, in-laws, everyone is expected to be there, no excuses.

The party is Saturday evening. Our fridge bulges with groceries from the Asian market, Mom working all week to hone her best recipes, including her famous braised beef and daikon dish.

Mom's side of the family are the Hungs, and for her three brothers and their families, everything is a competition. Their kids, their life, their stuff—against ours.

Always, Mom has had Carmen, Grandma's favorite, to show off at the party. But this year, there are only secrets to hide, Carmen's drastic change in appearance to explain.

Friday afternoon, I draw the heavy white drapes across our front windows, flick on the living room floor lamp, and set my music stand beside the upright piano.

Heading down the hall, I check the temperature on the downstairs thermostat, the tea steeping on the kitchen counter. Black, no sugar. Just the way Mr. Bergamaschi likes it.

At five minutes to four, I carefully tune my violin and flip through the first few pages of the second movement of the Bartók concerto, stopping at the section I'm least confident about. I have just enough time to play it through once before my lesson.

Setting the metronome, I count off the beats. Draw my bow over the strings.

But I can't hear myself think, can't hear myself play. I can't hear anything except the Japanese techno pounding from Carmen's room.

I tighten my grip on the bow and stare harder at the notes on the page. I need this time. I need this space. Carmen used to play the piano under the tutelage of an equally exacting teacher. She should understand.

I pound up the stairs and knock loudly on her door, taken aback by my own intensity.

"*What*"—Carmen yanks open the door, her eyes red and watery, her prickly bleached hair sticking up in all the wrong places—"the *hell*, Nina."

Her room, her breath, reek of smoke. But I don't budge from her door.

"I'm *trying to practice*," I say, my throat tight, fists clenched. In the back of my head, I'm wondering what Grandma would say if she saw Carmen looking like this.

"Okay." Carmen's lips twitch as if amused. "Then practice."

"Can you turn down your music?"

Her gaze drops to my clenched fists. "No."

"My lesson starts in a minute. Mr. Bergamaschi's particular about background noise."

"That old man hasn't retired yet?" Carmen throws her hands up in disbelief. I can't help but notice the raw patches of eczema around her knuckles, the cracked fingernails—a musician's nightmare. "How long are you going to hang on to his every word? Don't you get it, Nina? There's no point. Mom had me playing the piano for twelve years. *Twelve years.*" Carmen leans in close. "What's it done for me? Nothing."

I want to tell her that Mr. Bergamaschi is an excellent teacher. I'm fortunate to be his student and he's hard on me because he cares. But I figure my words would be wasted.

"So you're turning down your music?" I press.

"I don't have to do anything."

The doorbell chimes.

"Carmen, *please*," I ask one more time, hating the pleading note in my voice.

But she just shakes her head, retreating back into her room and closing the door.

28

I STAND IN front of my mirrored closet door, dabbing concealer on the sides of my nose, my chin, and left cheek.

Stepping back, I assess my new red blouse with the scoop neck and billowy sleeves that seems to soften my shoulders. I'm wearing my dark blue jeans today, hoping they make my legs look just a little slimmer. My hair hangs in big, loose curls. The result of trading my flat iron for my curling iron at the last minute.

I carefully smooth a hand over my hair, feeling a sharp pang in my chest. Regret that Ethan's not here to see me all dressed up, with my curls.

"Can someone *please* call Carmen?" Mom yells as she rushes out the door juggling a large pot of her braised beef stew with daikon and a platter of her Chinese mushroom and bok choy dish.

I know Mom's talking to me since Dad's in their bedroom, changing his tie and blazer for the third time on her orders.

I head down the upstairs hall and rap lightly on Carmen's door, bracing myself for whatever's on the menu today. "Carmen."

She cracks her door open, an inch, maybe two. "*What*, Nina?"

Hostility today, with a side of suspicion. Lovely.

"We're leaving," I announce, but my voice is flat. I don't feel like showing up to Grandma's either. Subjecting myself to her inspection, playing the comparison game with my aunts and uncles. But no one is excused.

The crack in the door widens another couple of inches. Carmen stands there with her bleached hair matted, no makeup, wearing sweatpants and a long-sleeved shirt.

"I'm not going," she growls, like I'm the one trying to force her to go.

"What do you mean?" Obviously, she still needs to get ready and we're going to have to wait and make up time on the road if we can. But there is no way we can leave without her.

"Just what I said."

"You can't *not* go. Everyone's going to ask why you aren't there. What are we supposed to say?"

"I guess"—Carmen shrugs like she's forgotten she's the one up on the pedestal, Grandma's favorite—"they'll just have to deal."

I blink, wondering who this person is, standing in front of me. I don't recognize my sister in her at all.

"Where's Carmen?" Mom looks up from her phone as I approach Dad's Mercedes, alone.

"She says she isn't coming."

"She w*hat?*" Mom throws open the passenger side door and heads back up the walk, a note of panic in her voice. "I *told* her to get ready an hour ago and we're already running late!"

"Mel," Dad says, coming out the front door. "Does this tie match?" But Mom brushes past him without a word.

Dad slides into the front seat of his car. There's muted

shouting from upstairs, but he doesn't seem to notice as he answers emails on his tablet.

His phone buzzes with an incoming call. Dad cancels it, but whoever it is calls again.

I recognize that agitated tone on the other end of the phone as soon as Dad picks up. Rich's words run into and over each other, no breaks. He's a fire hose of unfiltered thought punctuated with the occasional expletive.

"Rich." Dad tilts his head back, pinches the bridge of his nose. The torrent of words on the other end of the line remains unchecked. "*Rich.* I'm heading out to my in-laws. Yes, with the whole family. I'll call you back tomorrow morning. Right. I know. Talk to you then."

"Let's go, Vin," Mom orders, getting back in the car.

Dad turns to look in the back seat. "But what about—"

"She's not coming," Mom answers, yanking on her seat belt, and there's a tremor in her voice that makes my stomach turn.

Dad's jaw tightens as he eases the car down the driveway and onto the street. I see him glance at the house as we pull away, as if hoping Carmen will somehow change her mind and join us.

I put in my earbuds, pull up Bartók's Violin Concerto No. 2 on my phone, and bump up the volume. Closing my eyes, I picture my fingers pressing against the strings, the shifting angles of my bow. But somehow my fingering is off, the piano accompaniment running ahead. I try to keep up. I can't keep up.

It's easy, Nina. I hear Carmen's voice, speaking to me in a memory. *Clap right. Clap left. Clap backs of hands together. Clap palms together. Clap. Got it?*

It's the night of Grandma's party eleven years ago. We head west on Interstate 80, passing the produce stand with its hand-painted signs, fields and orchards stretching far out into the horizon. I ride in the back seat of Dad's old Mitsubishi with Carmen. She's a sophisticated eight and I'm six.

A plain, awkward six.

Now faster. Carmen urges. *Come on, Nina. Keep up!*

I want to keep up. I want to please. But I'm going left when she goes right. Mixing it up, slowing us down. I wish I could be eight. I wish I could be different, more like Carmen, less like me.

I stare out the window at the darkening sky, the shades of blue and gray. Mom tugs at her coat, leans forward, fidgeting with the heat settings. Dad sighs, rubbing the back of his neck as he studies the string of red taillights in front of us.

I've always acknowledged the gap—in years, in looks, in worlds—between me and Carmen. But never realized how much it meant to have someone to look up to. A sister to set the pace, to urge me on, to show me what was possible.

And Carmen made everything look possible. Except for the last thing any of us expected from her—failure.

29

WE FINALLY EXIT the freeway and wind slowly up a steep hill. Turn down one narrow street after another. There are no streetlights, and tall hedges and trees crowd the road. The houses grow larger, still larger. Gated properties with a view.

I run my fingers lightly through my curls, check the zit coming up on my left cheek, the other one on my chin. Already, I can feel Grandma's scrutinizing gaze, hear her sharp criticism of my skin. She'll accuse me of gaining weight. Again.

In the dark, we almost miss the turn onto a steep, private drive that takes us up still higher on the hill. It levels out into an enormous circular driveway packed with Teslas, Audis, Mercedes, and BMWs. Grandma's mansion rises in front of us, all three stories lit up. Clean white stucco, tall, rectangular windows, arched double doors set behind thick, white columns. My gaze sweeps to the left and right as I follow my parents up the marble steps.

"You're late," Grandma says, swinging open the heavy front door. Behind her, the party is in full swing. I hear the clack of mahjong tiles being shuffled and stacked and someone singing karaoke to a Mandopop song.

Mom nudges me forward for the obligatory hug. Somehow in my halting, rusty Mandarin, I find all the words to wish Grandma a happy New Year and a happy birthday.

"Nina." Grandma grips me by my shoulders and peers hard at my face. "Your skin is not good and you're getting fat."

I squirm, trying not to let her words and suffocating perfume get to me. I didn't choose to break out right before her party. Not to mention Grandma's idea of "fat" is any body shape other than rectangle—narrow hips, small waist. Funny thing is, she's more of a pear shape herself.

"Your hair, Melanie!" Grandma exclaims now, turning to Mom. "So much gray."

Mom winces, her hand creeping up to her styled hair. Sure, I've seen a couple silver threads, but they're hardly noticeable.

"And Vincent." Grandma's lips are pursed as she pins Dad with a sharp look, and I already know it's going to be about the startup. "Tell me the bad news. I hear the numbers are down."

Before Grandma can turn back to me, I take the platter of mushrooms and bok choy from Mom and slip inside the door.

It's strange, walking in without Carmen. I'm so used to her taking the spotlight—everyone exclaiming over her impeccable style, her long, shimmering hair, her glowing skin. Without her, I feel exposed, awkward.

"Nina!" Vivian, Uncle Edward's wife, booms as I step into the marble foyer. She's wearing a bright red Coach dress with a silk scarf and jade necklace, sipping a tapioca milk tea. "There you are! Better late than never."

Vivian and Edward have two kids, my cousins Wendy and Owen.

"Hi, Aunty," I say, changing out of my black oxfords and into one of the many pairs of house slippers by the door.

She peers behind me to where Grandma is still quizzing my parents. "So, where's Carmen?" she asks. "We missed her over the holidays. She must be busy, in her second year of college."

I nod. *Right, busy.*

I think of Carmen, standing behind her cracked door, her bleached hair matted and skin blotchy, her sweatpants and a long-sleeved shirt hiding the new weight around her waist, her thighs. Maybe it's best she didn't come.

"You're heading to college this fall too," Aunt Vivian continues. "What major are you applying for? How'd you do on your SATs?"

"I'd like to study music," I offer, carefully. Carmen was a master at navigating these conversations, neatly turning them away from herself and onto more neutral topics. But I find myself stuck like a target at a gun range.

"Music," Aunt Vivian repeats. "Not much money in that. Better to pick something more concrete. Owen and Wendy are both looking to go into the medical field like their dad."

"That's great," I say. The covered platter in my hands grows heavier by the second.

"Yes, a solid choice," Aunt Vivian agrees, though I question how much choice my cousins really have. "Anyways, Nina. You were telling me how you did on the SATs?"

I was not, actually.

"Nina!" Uncle Nelson interrupts, coming up and giving me a crushing side hug. He and my aunt Kate have three boys, Michael, Wes, and Jordan. Today, my uncle is sporting a Louis Vuitton blazer paired with Ralph Lauren Purple Label trousers. "Is that your mother's braised beef and daikon?" he asks, peering under the cover.

"Mushrooms, actually. Mom has the beef and daikon."

"Good!" Uncle Nelson rubs his hands and grins, showing off his blindingly white teeth. "I've been experimenting with the same recipe myself and I think it's time we had an official taste test. My recipe versus your mother's."

I nod, easing my way around my aunt and uncle. "I . . . better get this dish over to the kitchen."

Repositioning my grip on the platter, I head toward the monstrous kitchen with its custom cabinets, built-in refrigerators, and large dining area. But as I pass the mahjong tables, Uncle Alex looks up. He's single with two kids, Clarissa and Brandon, and tonight, he's wearing a crisp white dress shirt with the sleeves rolled up and gray Armani slacks.

"Nina, you're late!" he calls. "Did you see my new Cybertruck out there?"

I nod. "Pretty cool." Every time I see Uncle Alex he has a different car.

"So, where's Carmen?" he asks. "We'll need her to play us something on the piano later."

He's talking about the mandatory musical talent show at the end of the night where my cousins and I play our best pieces.

I remember Carmen playing Grandma's baby grand piano just last year. Her fingers flying up and down the keys, her right foot working the pedal. Dad's arm around Mom's shoulders. Everyone in the room leaning in, rapt.

Grandma's other instruments include a cello, a flute, a violin, a viola, even a Chinese zither my cousin Wendy could play at one time.

"She's not able to make it," I answer as casually as I can.

"That's a good one, Nina." Uncle Alex chuckles, turning back to his mahjong game.

I don't bother to correct his assumption, figuring he'll eventually find out for himself.

I finally make it to the kitchen. Dropping off Mom's dish, I start loading up a plate from the groaning kitchen islands, making sure to snag two pieces of Uncle Nelson's homemade scallion pancakes. In years past, Carmen and I would try to take a little of everything and split pieces of dessert when we were well past full.

My cousins are sitting at the big table in the dining area. Clarissa, Brandon, Wes, and Jordan are playing *Heads Up!* Michael and Owen are watching anime on Owen's phone and Wendy is just scrolling on hers.

"Hey," I say, taking the open seat beside Wendy.

She barely looks up—I remember Mom saying something about social anxiety and my Aunt Vivian signing her up for therapy. News that isn't being shared, at any rate, with Grandma.

Brandon beckons me to move to the other side of the table. "We can play with teams of three with you and Carmen."

"Actually," I hedge, "it's just me today."

"No Carmen?" Brandon asks and now everyone at the table except Wendy is looking at me.

I shake my head, shrinking under their questioning gaze. "Nope."

Just outside the kitchen, I hear Uncle Nelson discussing his latest business venture. His and Kate's recent move to a different neighborhood so their boys could be in a more competitive school district. The tennis court under construction in their new backyard.

There's no arriving with the Hungs— just the next thing and the next.

It won't be long before all of us at this table will be pulled into their conversations. Our test scores, our extracurriculars, our latest awards and achievements brought out into the open and compared one against the other.

I feel a tightness in my stomach thinking of Carmen's dismissal and the loss of my lead role in the string quartet. Two blows Mom will have to keep hidden.

I wish it didn't matter. But here, it does.

CATAN!!!!!! Roger's text flashes on my watch.

See above.

Did I mention Catan?!

Roger's hosting a game night tomorrow. I think of the Kishimoto's small, square, cookie-cutter house and smile, remembering that warm feeling of sitting down at their cluttered kitchen table with Carmen and Roger. Eating Mrs. Kishimoto's snickerdoodles and chugging tall glasses of oat milk, knowing I wouldn't get in trouble if I left crumbs on the table, took another cookie, or spilled my milk.

No comparisons, no expectations.

I'll be there, I type back.

30

I SPEND ALL Sunday afternoon in the living room practicing the second movement of my Bartók concerto.

By the time five o'clock rolls around, I'm more than ready to put my violin and sheet music away.

I head upstairs to see if Mom can give me a ride to Roger's for game night. Or better yet, let me drive her car while she sits in the passenger seat.

I'm surprised to find excitement building inside of me. Ethan was never one for board games and it's been far too long since I last played—or more accurately, dominated—Catan. Even the thought of Lucy being there doesn't dampen my resolve.

Outside my parents' room, I hear Mom and Dad's voices rising from just behind their cracked door.

"What does Carmen need the keys for?" Mom demands. Things are always tense between my parents after a trip to Grandma's, when the comparisons and criticisms are all still fresh. Uncle Nelson edging out Mom's best dish. Uncle Alex sharing that Clarissa's Academic Decathlon team is going to Nationals in May. Aunt Kate adding that Michael and Wes made the varsity team for tennis.

"It's *her* car, Mel." Dad's voice is terse. I remember him hedging questions about the growth of his startup last night in the wake of Uncle Edward announcing the opening of a second location for his dialysis clinic.

"We make the payments," Mom counters. "She won't see a counselor. She won't work on her community college applications. She won't even consider volunteer positions. She isn't getting the keys until she can show us she has a plan."

Grandma had held Carmen's absence against Mom all night. Even my performance of Romance No. 2 in F Major for Grandma's musical talent show at the end of the evening didn't change a thing.

"She's still trying to figure things out," Dad argues.

Turning quickly, I backtrack down the hall before I can hear Mom's reply. As I pass Carmen's room, I notice her door is shut and the lights are off. When we arrived home late last night, she was wandering outside in the backyard, the light of her phone bobbing in the dark. Pacing. Stopping only to study Mom's rose bushes though it's too early for blooms.

Everything feels off, unstable. Our elevated standing with Grandma suddenly in jeopardy. I feel the pressure, heavy and unrelenting. This need to right things as soon as possible, salvage our reputation whatever it takes.

Next time, I text Roger, even though I know he'd come pick me up if I asked.

I head back downstairs. Passing through the kitchen, I push open the sliding glass doors and step out into the backyard.

Everything is immaculate, the way Mom likes to keep it.

She designed the whole space when we first moved in. Hired one contractor to put in the large paver patio and build the pergola, another contractor to set out trees along the perimeter, install the small lawn and a low-maintenance water feature. The coral garden roses she special ordered, planting them herself while Dad set up his new propane grill.

When everything was finally finished, my parents talked about having the Kishimotos over to grill out, sit on the patio, kick around a soccer ball the way we used to when we lived on the same street.

But instead, everything just sat untouched. The fancy wicker furniture and tables, the new propane grill, all hidden under heavy dust covers.

It wasn't always like this. There was a time when life was different, slower, good. Back when we were neighbors with the Kishimotos, when our patio furniture was plastic and we only had one car.

In the summer afternoons Mom, Mrs. Kishimoto, Carmen, Roger, Roger's little brothers, and I would go to the community pool. Once we got through the locker room showers, Roger's little brothers would dash to the kiddie pool, our moms following at a slower pace. They'd find lounge chairs to lay out on and flip through home magazines and talk.

Roger, Carmen, and I would trek in the opposite direction to the big pool. Jump off diving boards, attempt handstands in the water, and race in the lap pool.

"Marco!" Roger would yell at random times throughout the afternoon. No lead-up, no warning. Starting a game just because.

Camen and I knew what was expected. "Polo!" we'd answer and scatter, before he could tag us.

Later in the afternoon, *they'd* show up. A group of older guys going into ninth and tenth grade. Tanned, muscled, with arrogant smiles, they would draw Carmen away from us, off to the deep end where they'd stay for hours hanging off the island in the middle of the pool. Splashing, talking, making it clear that the island was teenagers only.

Roger and I would swim as close to them as we dared, straining to hear their conversations. At least until Carmen caught sight of us and we'd have to duck and dive.

I was starting to realize that Carmen was growing up and branching out, the gap between us widening. The thought made me sad. But as I dove deep and swam fast to make my getaway, I looked over to find Roger right beside me. Diving deep, swimming fast. I couldn't explain then that feeling in my chest, warm and strong. Except that it kind of felt like climbing into the bed-boat, of having someone there, close.

I could always look over and find him there.

Much later, we'd finally head home, sunburnt and smelling of chlorine, ready to blunt that gnawing, ravenous hunger brought on by a day at the pool. We'd tumble out of the Kishimotos' big green minivan to the sweet, smoky smell of barbeque wafting from our backyard. Dad grilling steaks and Mr. Kishimoto making his famous teriyaki chicken on our old kettle grill.

We'd eat, talk, kick around a soccer ball until the sun set, the stars came out, and the crickets started their nightly racket.

I miss those summer nights. Miss being together with my family, with the Kishimotos. I miss Mr. Kishimoto and his big laugh and his teriyaki chicken.

The day Mr. Kishimoto had his massive heart attack, I

was out on our driveway taking out the recycling. He passed by, driving Roger's little brothers to school in their big green minivan. He waved and I waved back.

Then later that day, we got the news.

The hospital visits, the rapid decline, the funeral. Mom helping Mrs. Kishimoto settle his affairs, and in the middle of it all, we moved and everything just . . . changed.

Our lives became more regimented, less spontaneous. As if by cutting out everything fun or extraneous, we could control the uncontrollable. The irreversible.

As if.

31

THERE'S A SUBTLE shift in our house, an unspoken understanding.

Over the next two weeks, Mom gets her hair professionally dyed, concealing the hardly noticeable gray Grandma found so unacceptable. Dad puts in even longer hours, as if to prove Grandma wrong about the future of his startup. I work harder on the Bartók concerto for my senior recital, knowing Grandma and my aunts, uncles, and cousins will all be in attendance and I can't fail in front of them. It has to be perfect.

Katheryn still hasn't responded to my request to meet. I wonder if it got lost in her emails. At school, I see Bea in the halls. But she doesn't approach me, doesn't engage, and I'm just fine with that.

Every time I pass Carmen's door, it's closed and her light is off. It isn't until I'm getting ready for bed that I hear her stirring, talking on the phone, telling whoever is waiting for her outside that she'll be right there.

Reminders pop up on my phone for a fundraising event, a corporate party. Gigs for the string quartet I should be leading. But I'm out completely, done. Just like Carmen.

On the way to orchestra, I stop in front of Ethan's mural, pretending to study the lines and colors and details. But inside I'm falling. Inside I'm sinking into deep, dark, cold water.

Somewhere down in the deep, down in the dark, is Ethan. The version I never got to know. To find him, I have to swim. I have to dive deeper. Down past the fence lines of our bikes, the mural, the orchestra shirts. Deeper still, past the *someone else* Bea had hinted at. The arrest, the suspension, the rehab—"history," as Jayden referred to it.

I'm far deeper than I've gone before. It's cold down here as I peer in the dark, searching for him.

Can I see you?

His text to me when I was at YMI. These four words that opened the way for us to begin again.

And it *was* different. Our messages more raw, more real. I told Ethan things I didn't tell Mom when she called to check on me. Things like how inferior I felt among my peers at YMI. How hard I was being pushed and challenged and tested by my instructors. It wasn't what I thought it would be, and all I could think about was how poorly I stacked up against everyone else around me—

Don't think, Ethan had texted back. **Just do.**

Getting out of my head. Narrowing my view to just me, just my violin, and what I could do. It changed everything for me at YMI.

Ethan seemed to be in a low. But instead of shutting down, closing himself off, his messages back were immediate and lengthy. Telling me his biggest fear was change. That with graduation looming, it felt like the future was knocking on his door whether he was ready or not. Perhaps he should have applied to those art schools. But it was too late now.

We can figure out other options, I'd texted, my mind already turning over ideas, **when I get back.**

It felt like anything was possible, now that the rift between us was mended.

See you tomorrow? I'd texted, the night I got back from YMI. It was a rhetorical question really. I was certain I'd see him. Tomorrow, the next day, and the next.

I am searching now in the deep, in the dark for the Ethan who biked to the bridge that night. In such unbearable pain, that in that moment he considered death a better option than life.

What if I had tried to see him that night? Would it have changed anything?

I'm shivering, shaking, running out of air. I look up at the surface but it seems so far away. I'm not ready to abandon my search. But my lungs are burning, summoning me back to the world up top.

IT'S ELEVEN-THIRTY AT night and I am still working on stats homework. I am flipping through the textbook, looking for a specific formula, when I hear it. Carmen's door opening and closing, her footsteps on the stairs. But instead of the front door opening, I hear the rumble of the garage door.

Peering out my window, I watch as Carmen backs her car down the driveway and disappears into the night.

The next morning, Carmen's room is empty, her car still gone.

A knot of anger tightens in my stomach. All she seems to do is take. It's her keys, her car, her life.

I head downstairs for breakfast. Dad is sitting on one of the barstools at the island, eating a bagel, his tablet and a cup of coffee on the countertop beside him.

"Where's Mom?" I ask, rummaging through the fridge for the strawberry jam.

Her briefcase isn't by the kitchen island, and I don't see her pot of organic steel-cut oats on the stove.

"She's still getting ready." Dad glances up from his tablet and then back down. He reaches for his coffee.

I fight the urge to nod and move on, my default when it comes to conversations with Dad. I've never had the chumminess Carmen shared with him growing up, the easy flow of words from all the rides to and from volleyball practices and games. With Mom taking me to violin recitals and competitions, I never really had much one-on-one time with him before the startup took over his life.

But right now, I can't stand the way he's acting. Like there's nothing wrong with him giving Carmen privileges that Mom has firmly opposed.

"I saw Carmen leave last night," I say, cutting myself a thick slice of the sourdough loaf Mom picked up from the farmer's market two days ago. Spread on a thick layer of jam.

Dad glances up from his tablet, his expression neutral.

"I thought Mom said she couldn't have the keys," I press, wanting him to own up to his role in all this. "That she wasn't responsible enough."

Carmen is part of the equation to right things with Grandma. But it seems like he doesn't want to acknowledge that. The same way he doesn't seem to want to acknowledge anything about Ethan—back then or now.

"I don't see how this is any of your concern," Dad snaps, tipping back the last of his coffee.

I flinch, feeling my face grow hot, then hotter.

"Anyways," Dad says, getting up to set his plate and mug in the sink. "Your mom should be down any minute. I'm heading to work."

I nod, hoping he doesn't see the redness in my cheeks, the tears smarting the corners of my eyes.

32

THE SEASONS CHANGE. The days get warmer but windier and the heavy cloud cover dissipates.

I move through the halls, my head down and arms crossed. Fighting the wind that whips the trees and chaps my face. In spite of my petitions, my biking privileges haven't been reinstated. But on days like this, I'm glad I ride with Roger.

The wind blows food wrappers out of trash cans and rips flyers and posters from the walls. A flyer slaps against my leg. SENIOR CLASS PHOTO FRIDAY! it reads, and the graphics are basic, ordinary. Just like the school's new resident artist. 11 O'CLOCK AT THE FOOTBALL FIELD.

Ethan would have turned this flyer into something eye-catching, a work of art. It all seems like a dream now, those days when I could sit beside him in the graphic arts room, watch him create. Now, I notice art in a way I never did before.

"They're taking the senior class photo with a drone," Lucy chatters on the car ride home with Roger. "What do you plan to wear, Nina? Do you know where you're going to stand?"

"I'm not sure," I say, my words clipped. Even though it's been almost six weeks, I still can't wrap my head around the fact that she got me kicked off the string quartet, took over my role as lead.

"Stand with us," Roger urges. "We're planning to wear highlighter yellow so we can really *pop*."

"Pretty sure I don't have that color in my closet." I *definitely* don't. Mom would freak.

Back in my room, I pull out my physics textbook and try to make some headway studying for the test on Friday. There's something about physics that doesn't make sense to me. Though it should, with all its laws of motion and everything governed by an equation.

If anything, I understand structure. I grew up with Mom's Basic Rules. I didn't have to wonder what was expected of me. Things were pre-determined and if I followed the plan, I'd succeed. The way I need to succeed now.

My phone buzzes.

"Nina." Mom's voice is strangely high, tight. "Is Carmen home?"

"I'm not sure." Her room was dark and silent when I passed by earlier. I had assumed Carmen was just sleeping, recovering from another long night out. "Why?"

"The police found her car."

"*What?* Where?" I hear the rising panic in my voice as I jog out of my room and down the hall to Carmen's.

"It was in a ditch," Mom says, in the same strange, high pitch. "By the university."

I rap hard on Carmen's door. *Please, be home. Please be okay.* When I don't hear her grudging "*What?*" I try the knob and her door swings open, revealing the pigsty.

I feel a twinge of guilt as my gaze zeroes in on the blank spot on her wall where Ethan's sketch used to hang. She hasn't seemed to notice. But still, I know I need to return it.

"She's not in her room," I report back. As I pull her door

shut, I notice some empty pill bottles on the floor, half buried in the heaping piles of clothes. I didn't know she was on any medication—

"What about the bathroom?" Mom asks.

But she's not there or anywhere else in the house.

"Her phone's off," Mom says. "If she comes home, call me immediately."

"Okay."

I pace the downstairs hall after we hang up. Covering the space between the front door and the sliding glass door that leads out to the backyard. Back and forth, back and forth.

Fragments of images crowd my head. Her car veering off the road. Bumping down into a ditch. Her body flying forward, head snapping back. She could be anywhere right now, hurt or worse—

A key turns in the lock and the front door swings open.

I whirl around to find Carmen stepping into the foyer. Behind her, a black Nissan peels away from the curb and disappears down the street.

"Where *were* you?" The words were meant to be a question, but instead, I hear the accusation in my tone even as I search her face, her arms, looking for any visible injuries.

"Out," Carmen says, her eyes narrowing. She looks completely unscathed. "You have a problem with that?"

"Where's your car?" I ask, even though I know exactly where it is. The image of her losing control of the vehicle still shakes me.

Carmen shuts the door behind her and steps toward me, frowning. "Why do you care?"

I draw in a sharp breath, feeling a tidal wave of thoughts rising. Her vanishing act starting her senior year of high school. Academic probation in college, a lost volleyball scholarship. Her canceled trips home, the sudden change in her looks, her dismissal, and now this incident with her car—

I don't see how this is any of your concern. Dad's voice repeats in my head, reprimanding me.

I ignore it, thinking instead of Ethan, telling me his biggest fear was change. Perhaps I'm no different. Perhaps these changes in Carmen, both the subtle and the obvious, have scared me, have *been* scaring me.

"Because what you do affects me. It affects all of us!" I hear myself shout. Our family standing with Grandma in jeopardy. The pressure, heavy and unrelenting, to right things. "We had nothing to show at Grandma's, but everything to hide."

"Don't try to put that on me."

"Right." I almost laugh. "It's always everyone else's problem, isn't it? You never take the fall for anything."

Something shifts in her face, a flicker of hurt. Her lips tremble, her features softening and for a second, I'm reminded of a younger version of Carmen.

"Don't act like you know me, Nina." Carmen pushes past, the cold, hard mask back in place.

I start after her, reaching for her arm. Wanting to pull her back, tell her I'm glad she's okay, that I wish we could talk again, like we used to.

But instead, I drop my hand, letting her trudge up the stairs alone.

Then I pull out my phone and call Mom.

33

THERE'S A PHOTO on the mantle next to all our mandatory school pictures. Carmen posing on her eighteenth birthday in a purple sleeveless top and dark jean shorts that make her toned legs go on forever. She's got one hand on her hip, the other pressed against the hood of her new silver Mazda.

"First ride. I think I'll take Nina."

I remember sitting in that car, my back straight, knees pressed together, and hands clasped in my lap, not wanting to mess a thing up. I still couldn't believe that she chose me. Not our parents, not her friends, not her teammates. *Me.*

At a traffic light, a lifted Jeep pulled up beside us with four college boys. The one up front with the dark hair and olive skin flashed her a smile.

"Fire," I whispered, playing our old game. Wanting some kind of connection with Carmen before she left for college in a few weeks. But Carmen didn't seem to hear, or didn't want to play along.

They kept following us, the boys in the Jeep. To the next light and the next. I kept looking over, sneaking peeks. But Carmen just stared straight ahead, turning up the volume of her eclectic playlist like they didn't exist.

At the next intersection, she dropped them. Taking a right instead of going straight just as the light turned green.

We drove along tree-lined streets, passing grocery stores, a bank, apartments. On and on until there was nothing but sky above us and farm fields stretching away to the horizon.

I glanced over at my sister, admiring her smooth skin, her golden tan, the definition in her arms.

All school year she'd been busy with college applications and extracurriculars. Closed off and tight-lipped about whatever was bothering her. I thought we'd have the summer to reconnect. But instead, Mom enrolled me in online math and science camps with extra tutoring in reading comprehension and composition on the side. In spite of Carmen's protests, Mom had her working a summer internship at Dad's company to get some real-world experience.

Finally, here in Carmen's new car, it was just me, just her. Open fields, sky, road, a chance to really catch up on our lives. Yet we couldn't seem to find two words between us.

There were only the songs on the playlist, cycling one after another. Classic rock, electronic beats, country ballads. I resented this music taking the place of the conversations that used to flow so easily.

We headed north, then east, houses emerging up ahead, streetlights. In a few minutes, we'd be home.

As I pulled my gaze from my sister, I caught a glimpse of myself in the side-view mirror. Round face, low ponytail, skin that still broke out.

The same reflection I'd seen a thousand times. Yet this time, I felt a sinking realization. The girl in the side mirror could never be enough to bridge the gap between me and Carmen, in years, in looks, in worlds.

A gap I was now certain would only become more pronounced, more permanent with time.

34

AT NIGHT, I hear Mom and Dad's voices rising from their room.

"There's only minor body damage," Dad insists.

Carmen's car had slid off the road and spun around before tipping into the ditch at an impossible angle.

I slip downstairs and into the garage, drawn by the need to see, to know. I walk toward Carmen's car, parked on the far side of the garage. The silver shine is gone, the paint chipped and scratched, the front end of the car crumpled in.

My breath catches and all I can hear is the heavy thudding of my own heart. Just like that first day back after winter break when everything felt so *wrong*.

In my head, I picture myself as a bystander watching as Carmen's car swerves off the road. Through the windshield, I see Carmen's eyes widen, her mouth open in a scream as her car spins toward the ditch. I want to reach out and suspend time. Keep her from falling. But I'm stuck, helpless on the sidelines.

What was she doing just before she lost control? Was she texting, driving impaired?

Back in bed, I listen to the gusting wind and the creak of trees. Actions and reactions—isn't that part of Newton's third law of motion? Carmen's actions, her choices, where are they leading?

Somewhere in the distance, a train whistle.

I press my face into the pillow and scream. One long, silent scream.

35

THE FOLLOWING WEEK is quiet with Carmen lying low in her room, complying at least for the moment, with the rules of her grounding.

Dad is at the office early in the morning and stays until late at night, handling the company layoffs with Philip from research and development.

It was supposed to be Rich, not Philip, at Dad's side. But I hear Dad telling Mom that Rich is still tied up with his divorce proceedings, the division of property and debts. Available only in fits and spurts.

I have a paper in government to write, physics homework to complete, the third movement of my Bartók concerto to learn. But instead, I pick up the clear-view folder with Ethan's sketch and head down the hall to Carmen's room.

As usual, her light is off. I wonder if she's sleeping or just sitting in the dark.

"Carmen."

It seems to take her forever to open the door.

"What is it, Nina?" There are dark circles under her eyes and the corners of her lips are cracked.

I fidget with the folder in my hands before holding it out toward her. "I just . . . wanted to ask how you got this."

Carmen's eyes immediately narrow, her head swiveling

toward the place where Ethan's sketch used to hang on her wall. "How did *you* get it?"

I bite my lip, heat rushing to my face. "I saw it in your room, the night you asked me to find the tablet."

"So, you took it." A statement.

I bite my lip, force a nod. I can't meet her accusing gaze.

"Keep it," she snaps, hardly glancing at the sketch. "It means nothing to me."

Nothing to me.

The phrase echoes in my head as I walk down the hall, back into my room, and shut the door. I return Ethan's sketch to its place on my desk. It's mine now, I guess. But somehow, I don't feel very happy about it.

Opening my laptop, I work on my government paper for an hour before switching to my physics homework. The whole time, I feel the four walls of my room closing in on me. Closer and closer—

"Nina." Mom raps loudly on my door.

"Yeah?" I get up to pull the door open before she can just let herself in.

"Your dad's working late tonight," Mom says, glancing down as a message pops up on her watch. "I'm heading to the Co-op to pick up some groceries."

"Can I come?" I hear myself ask. The idea of running errands with Mom isn't appealing, but I just need to go somewhere, *anywhere* that's not here.

Mom looks past me to the open laptop on my desk, my textbooks, calculator, notepad. "Where are you with your assignments?"

"Making progress," I say, invoking one of my standard answers to Mom's interrogations.

"What about your piece for the senior recital?" she presses.

"Coming along."

She studies my face, her jaw tight and lips pressed in a straight line. "Fine," she says, her tone reluctant. "Let's go then."

The parking lot at the Davis Food Co-op is busy, the bike racks full.

"You have to be careful in these kinds of situations," Mom cautions, maneuvering around a car stopped with its blinker on. "There are cyclists, pedestrians, cars backing out . . . you don't want to move too quickly."

She's giving me driving tips, but not the steering wheel. I still have seven modules left in the defensive driving course she signed me up for. Though it seems like something Carmen should be taking, not me.

Mom finds a parking spot on the other end of the lot. We walk past the statue of a big tomato out front, the bistro tables, the racks of herbs. The automatic doors woosh open. Inside, I draw in a breath of all the fresh, spicy, earthy smells.

Carmen and I used to come with Mom all the time so we could pick out a honey stick or a treat from the bulk bins—usually strawberry yogurt granola or fig bars, the only kinds of snacks Mom allowed us to get.

Mom hands me a basket and points me to the back of the store. "Beef bone broth should be along those shelves. I also need one pound of organic steel-cut oats from the bulk bins and a bottle of coconut aminos. I'll pick up the lettuce and the rib eye."

I wander down the snack aisle on the way to the condiment section, basket banging against my thigh.

My gaze skims the shelves. Chips, crackers, dried fruit... granola bars. I freeze at the sight of a familiar blue box with white lettering. Ethan's go-to brand. The bars he always had shoved in the pockets of his jeans as he worked outside on the mural.

"Fuel," he'd called it, tearing open the wrapper and offering me the first bite.

Something tightens inside of me at the memory, a sharp stab of pain.

Each day that passes is another wedge, another gap between where Ethan's life ended and where mine continues. I don't like all that space. I want him *here*, now, with me. Not in my past.

The indie folk music playing through the ceiling speakers irritates me. I force myself to keep moving down the aisle and into the condiment section. There are too many different bottles on the shelves, too many labels to look at. I'm drained before I even start my search.

I had wanted a change of scenery. Something other than my laptop screen, the four walls of my room. But now that I'm here, out in the noise, surrounded by people, I just want to go home.

"Nina," Mom chides as we stand in the check-out line. "This is not the right brand." Reaching around me, she plucks the bottle of coconut aminos off the conveyor belt.

"They all had the same ingredients, so I didn't think it mattered." I know better than to defend myself, but I do it anyway.

Mom shakes her head. "Sourcing matters. I need to swap this out. Excuse me."

She heads back into the store. I feel curious glances from

those in line behind me. Biting my lip, I face forward, a flush creeping into my cheeks.

"Ma'am." The checker offers a sympathetic smile. It only makes me feel worse. "Did you bring your own bags?"

I nod, handing them over. But my attention is fixed on someone behind him.

Long, thin features, gray bob, rimless specs, a faded green skirt suit. Dr. Katheryn Travvers sits at a booth near the front windows, her laptop open in front of her, a mug of tea and a box from the hot food station beside her.

I watch as she lifts the tea mug, her thin lips folding over the rim as she sips, swallows. I watch her page down on her document, reading, absorbing, her expression focused and impassive. Something churns inside of me—

"Excuse me. One more item." Mom reappears, handing the new bottle of coconut aminos to the checker and tapping her card to pay. "Let's go, Nina."

But instead of grabbing our cart and pushing it out of the store, I walk straight back to the booths.

"Dr. Travvers." My voice shakes, and I feel those wrenching fingers once again in my chest.

Katheryn's blue eyes widen, then narrow. She sets her mug down.

"What is it, Nina?" she asks, and her voice is strained.

"Did you get my message asking to meet?" The email I sent almost eight weeks ago. The one she never bothered to dignify with a response.

"I did," she says, her tone unapologetic.

"Is there a time that works for you?" I ask, fumbling for my phone so I could pull up my calendar app. "I'd still like to talk."

All I want is for her to help me understand who Ethan was. In the same plain language I admired so much from her publications.

"No." Katheryn's gaze is cold, unblinking.

"I just want to understand—"

Her face tightens. "*You* need to understand," she says slowly, "that Ethan would still be here today, if it weren't for people like you."

People like me.

Me.

I hear Mom's footsteps approach, her voice calling my name.

But I can't move, can't think, can't breathe. I'm stuck on the bridge, feeling the weight of the approaching train pressing against my chest, the rocking rhythm of its axles in my jaw.

I could scream, but the whistle screams louder.

A hand clamps over my shoulder.

"What are you doing over here, Nina?" Mom demands, steering me toward the exit as Katheryn turns away.

36

I STAND IN front of Ethan's mural, my finger tracing the lines and details he painted so carefully.

People like you, Katheryn had said.

What, exactly, did she mean by that? Was she implying it was me, my fault? Or was she talking about someone else? Someone "like" me?

I blink quickly, trying to swallow past the thickness in my throat, but a tear slips down my cheek. My request to meet wasn't too much, too soon. Not only did Katheryn not want to meet with me, she possibly even held me responsible.

"You come here a lot?"

Quickly I swipe the tear from my cheek as Bea walks up beside me in a black leather skirt and tall combat boots. The last time we talked, I was backed up against a trash can, her finger in my chest, as she told me I didn't know Ethan *at all*.

"Yeah," I finally say, staring straight ahead, my finger still tracing the lines of the mural.

"Me too."

I glance over quickly, surprised at the raw sadness in her tone. Wonder what kind of game she's playing with me this time.

Bea tilts her head up, her gaze sweeping from one side of the mural to the other, taking it all in. "Pretty incredible."

"He was," I answer, even though I know she's referring to the mural.

"Jayden told me—" Her eyes dart toward me. "That you had asked him a while back about Ethan. About what was going on with him."

My finger freezes on the mural and I let it fall as I turn to face her.

"What about it?" The back of my neck prickles and my muscles tense, wary.

Bea looks down at her hands, then back up at me. There are dark patches on her knuckles where scabs had been before. "It's good," she says simply, and again her tone throws me, "for you to know all of him."

I shake my head. "I still don't feel like I do." Our lengthy message string leading up to that last text when I asked if I would see him tomorrow. Did that *someone else* know what he was going to do?

"Count yourself lucky," Bea says as the warning bell sounds and she steps away. "You got to see his best side. He didn't show that to everyone."

But I don't feel lucky. I feel left out. Like I wasn't someone he trusted enough with the—

"Get to class!" the vice principal calls, as she walks up from the parking lot.

I startle, my hand tightening on the handle of my violin case. I turn away from the mural, my eyes grazing the bottom right corner, where his trademark signature, "E.T.," should be. But it's not.

The orchestra room is buzzing by the time I take my seat. A nervous energy charges the air. College decision letters have been coming in all month, but now it's the last week of March. Today must be Ivy Day—the day Ivy League schools release their admission decisions.

Beside me, Lucy emits a high-pitched squeal. I try to ignore her, but she's jumping, screaming, holding her phone. "I got in! I got in! I got in!"

I've heard of lottery winners going crazy, unable to turn off their initial excitement. Institutionalized, ultimately. I should probably warn her, but instead I'm thinking about Ethan's mural, those missing initials.

A harsh reminder that he never completed "The Final Push."

Guilt lodges in my throat. Was it because of me? My excitement over leaving for YMI, not knowing his dislike for change, his history with people leaving him? Or was it because he already knew then, what he was going to do?

His mural, his life, unfinished. Nothing about this is right.

"YOU HAVEN'T HEARD back?" Mom quizzes me later that day as she takes the whites out of the washing machine and loads them into the dryer. "How is that possible?"

I shrug, handing her the basket of the dark-colored clothes I sorted. Half of the clothes in the basket are Carmen's but she hasn't come out of her room to help despite Mom's multiple requests.

"I've been checking my email—" I begin.

"You must have gotten *something*," Mom insists. "You know, Brenda's daughter has been accepted to Princeton, her first-choice school."

"I know." It's obvious everything works out perfect for Lucy, hashtag "blessed."

"Colleges are getting more and more selective," Mom lectures as she reloads the washer and twists the dial settings. "In just the last five years alone, fewer Davis High students are getting into the UCs, the Ivy League schools."

One of Mom's favorite pastimes is to scour the college admissions articles every year, tracking trends.

"Carmen had the support of a college admissions counselor," Mom continues. She closes the laundry room door behind us and grabs the stick vacuum from the hall closet. "You could have had the same support," she stresses, powering on the machine. "But you were so sure you could do it yourself."

"I *did* do it myself," I mutter, feeling my face grow hot. Wishing she believed in me, the way Ethan had.

I put together my own applications, submitted my prescreen recordings, and picked which scholarships to apply for. I know it wasn't perfect, especially the rush in December to submit my music college applications. But surely it was good enough.

"What?" She frowns, trying to get the vacuum lines perfect on the carpet.

"I. Did. *Do it.*" I repeat, louder this time.

I hate that she's multitasking, as if our conversation isn't worth her full attention.

"Did *what?*" The suction is on turbo now. She's still vacuuming that same section of carpet, making sure each pass lines up exactly with the last.

I shake my head, backing down the hall and to my room.

37

THE REJECTION LETTERS come in waves. The first wave from five of the schools on Mom's pre-approved list and from two of the music colleges on my list.

I click from one email to the next, my head pounding, muscles tightening, a wail trapped in my throat.

The Admissions Committee has completed an exhaustive review process...

We regret we are unable to offer you a place in our freshman class...

All decisions are final...

We appreciate your interest...

Same words, same phrases, different letterheads. Carmen gets kicked out of school and now I can't get in. I hear Mom's voice in my head, chastising me. I sense her deep disappointment.

Tell me, how are you going to explain this?

I can't. Not to her. Not to Grandma. Not even to me.

Not real.

The mantra I've repeated ever since Ethan died. These two words that are supposed to shield me from the hurt, the pain.

Not real.

I'm thinking it, saying it. But it doesn't seem to change a thing.

Downstairs, the doorbell rings. Mr. Bergamaschi arriving for my violin lesson. With my shaky progress on the concerto, we're still doing sixty-minute lessons instead of forty-five.

"Stop, stop." Mr. Bergamaschi cuts me off with an irritated flick of his hand. "You are rushing this passage, skipping notes. Play it cleanly or don't play it at all."

Biting my lip, I reset my violin and reposition my fingers. Try again.

The passage is in the first movement of the Bartók concerto which is supposed to be polished and memorized by now. But I can't find the tempo or the notes and I still can't feel the music.

"That's enough." Mr. Bergamaschi leans forward, a frown embedded in his thick, unkempt beard. "Practice, practice, practice. I won't hear it until it's fixed. Let's go to the second movement."

Tears prick my eyes. I turn quickly, pretending to shuffle through my sheet music for the right pages.

It's two weeks until my senior recital and I'm playing like a first-year orchestra student instead of a thirteen-year veteran. I don't even have the excuse of being too busy with the string quartet since Lucy took over.

I flounder through the second movement and then the third.

Without even looking up, I can see the grimace twisting Mr. Bergamaschi's rough features. He's invested years into mentoring me, teaching me, and now this.

I'm done, it's over. There won't be a senior recital. Mom

will have to cancel the reservation at the university performance hall, the bookings for the sound and video crew, the dessert caterer.

My senior recital, my college acceptance, building blocks that are supposed to help restore our family's standing with Grandma. My stomach knots at the thought of telling Mom that I'm failing on both fronts.

"Finish memorizing the third movement." Mr. Bergamaschi scribbles one last note in my lesson book and claps it shut. "Have your piano accompanist here next week and we'll do a full run-through."

That's it? That's all? Doesn't he have *something* to say about the tragedy of the last sixty minutes?

I take his empty tea mug to the kitchen and rush to grab his rumpled suit jacket from the hall closet. I walk him out the front door to his car, hoping for some final pointers, but he doesn't say a thing.

38

REJECTED.

Rejected.

Rejected.

Waitlisted.

Accepted.

They're in. The final wave of letters.

I'm accepted to a school on Mom's pre-approved list and waitlisted at the number two music college on my list.

"Two out of twelve applications." Mom shakes her head as she runs the duster over the piano. "That's not even twenty percent! And the waitlist is no guarantee, Nina."

"It's something." Everything. Going to a music college has been my dream. I *have* to go.

"You should have listened to me," Mom lectures. "A college admissions counselor would have made a big difference. This is not what I had hoped for you—"

Her phone buzzes on the coffee table. It's Grandma calling. She reaches for it, warning me with a look to stay where I am.

But I duck away. I don't need to hear everything I've heard before. Not when all my plans lie in shambles at my feet.

39

BACK WHEN ROGER, Carmen, and I were in elementary school, our families would go to the park on Saturday mornings so our parents could browse the farmer's market and we could ride the pedal-powered carousel. I always picked Fredrick the Frog and Roger would take Seymour the Seal beside me. I loved the bouncing music, that feeling of flying.

It's been years since I rode that carousel, but as the days tick down to my senior recital, I feel like I'm stuck on that ride. The operator pushes the bike pedals that make the animals go round and round, faster and faster. In the dizzy spin, my set plans and goals for music college and running the string quartet fall away, but I'm still on the ride and everything is in motion and I can't jump off. I don't know how.

In my room, I try on a vibrant blue satin dress with a sweetheart bodice and an A-line floor-length skirt. It's formal, elegant, expensive. Prom-worthy. Not that I'm going.

"I don't like it." I tug at the tight bodice and frown at my reflection in the mirrored closet door.

"Well, I'm not returning it," Mom says. "You had every chance to go shopping with me this weekend, but instead you—"

"It's strapless!" I point to the exposed skin beneath my collarbone. "You *know* I can't wear strapless!"

I can't play my senior recital in a strapless dress. It just won't work. Why is that so hard to understand?

"I *don't* know that. I've seen you wear similar styles—"

"With straps!"

"I don't see what the issue is here," Mom snaps. "This is the third and final dress. I'm done competing with all the last-minute prom dress shoppers."

"But I have shoulders!" I wail, catching another glimpse of myself in the mirror. "Shoulders!"

A message flashes on my watch. Two.

Keep it down.

Trying to sleep.

Carmen. Texting from her room after blowing off her community college classes.

"Yes." Mom raises her neatly groomed brows. She picks the garment bag off the floor and hangs it in my closet. "So do I."

As soon as she leaves, I pull down my old violin case from the top shelf in my closet. Taking out the black T-shirt, I crush it to my chest and sink to the floor. Let the tears fall freely down my face.

More than anything, I wish that Ethan was here to see me play. I wish we could have had the best of both worlds, where he supported my music and I supported his art. I wish he was still *alive*.

My fingers tighten against the fabric as a heavy weight bears down on me. This pressure to bottle up my grief and make everything work, the way Mom did all those years ago.

It's like I'm back in the weight room, planting my feet, throwing all my strength behind the bar. My arms shake and sweat pops on my forehead. I'm trying to straighten my arms, lift the bar, but it's too heavy. The weight of expectations. This crushing pressure to succeed.

The carousel ride spins, my senior recital approaches, and I'm afraid of getting up on that stage. Afraid that I will fail, like I've *been* failing.

That instead of rising, I'll fall.

40

THE FIRST CORAL blooms from Mom's prize garden roses are cut, gone. The bushes were naked this morning without their large, intricate flowers.

Carmen conveniently wasn't around for questioning. She'd left the house last night—breaking the rules of her grounding.

Country music blares from Annabel's speakers. Roger bumps up the volume another notch, hums along as we ride to school. Normally I would complain. But today, the music drowns out the memory of my parents arguing this morning, Mom furious, laying out her ultimatums.

I stare out the window at the cloudless sky, the green fields, the flowering trees. Everything bright, cheery, hopeful. All the things that I'm not.

"So," Roger says, glancing sideways at me. He's wearing his standard all-weather Kirkland shorts, an Honor Society T-shirt hanging loosely from his tall, thin frame. "Are you nervous?"

I open my mouth to answer. But the light turns red and Roger slams on the brakes, throwing me against the duct-taped dash.

"About your driving?" I grouch, picking my backpack up off the floorboard and straightening my cardigan. "Yeah."

Roger chuckles. "I meant your *big day*, your senior recital! You've only been working toward this since kindergarten."

"Right." I twist my hands in my lap, thinking about the Bartók concerto I still need to perfect, the music colleges I didn't get into, my recital dress sans straps.

"Mom and I will be there early on Friday," Roger continues. "To help with setup."

"Thanks." My voice is flat instead of grateful or excited, or whatever it is I should be feeling.

The RSVPs have been flooding in. My aunts, uncles, cousins, Grandma, family friends, my parents' coworkers. Everyone, it seems, except the one person I want most.

"I know you got a fancy dessert caterer lined up for the event," Roger rattles on. "But my mom said to tell you she's making a double-batch of snickerdoodles. Just for you."

I try to smile, remembering that warm feeling of sitting down at the Kishimotos' cluttered kitchen table, eating snickerdoodles and chugging tall glasses of oat milk. But instead, I feel my chin shake and tears start to fall.

"Nina." Roger glances over at me, his brow knitted. "Hey now."

His voice is familiar, kind. The way it's always been.

"Was it something I said?" he asks, as we pass the Little League fields.

I shake my head and reach up to swipe my nose, dab my eyes. "It's just—" I take a breath, trying to steady my voice. "Not what I imagined."

"Your senior recital? It hasn't even happened yet."

"Senior *year.*" My voice trembles and the tears start to fall again, harder, faster. I thought I'd be concertmistress, run the quartet, get accepted to my number one school. But turns out it is three for three for Lucy, not me.

She's even got a prom date. I thought I'd have one too this year but even that dream is dead.

We're almost at the high school, but Roger slows, turning into the parking lot of the community park with the arts center and the wooden play structure we used to pretend was a fort. He rummages for a travel pack of tissues in the back seat and passes them to me.

I blow my nose at least five times, using up almost the entire pack.

Beside me, Roger hedges, his dark eyes scanning my face. "Do you want to go for a walk?" he finally asks.

I stare back at him as we listen to the sound of the late bell ringing in the distance. I think of Mr. Martinez calling the orchestra to order, Lucy walking primly to the front of the room—

"Sure," I answer, tucking what is left of the tissue pack in the pocket of my cropped jeans.

We get out of the car and walk in silence along the paved path, looking at the grass running up the hills, the arching canopies of trees above us.

"Carmen's been home," I hear myself say.

"My mom mentioned something about that, but I haven't seen her around," Roger says. "Why isn't she in LA?"

"She was dismissed."

It feels wrong, saying this out loud to someone other than our immediate family. Like I'm telling secrets I shouldn't. But it's also a relief to admit it.

Roger shakes his head. "Not possible. Carmen's the all-star."

"Was," I correct. "She's different now. It's like she can't even stand us. She's always trying to leave the house. Meet up with friends at all hours of the night. She comes home disheveled, smelling like smoke—"

I break off, feeling myself tear up again.

"What happened?" Roger asks. "Did you try to find out?"

I think of the problem at the start of her senior year. Something she never told me about, and I never asked. How I stood downstairs with my parents after the secret of her dismissal was exposed. Instead of following her to her room, sitting with her as she cried. The way I reached out for her arm the day she slid her car into a ditch, only to let my hand drop instead.

"No," I answer, wincing at the memories. "Not really."

"Maybe," Roger says, as we approach the wooden play structure, "she needs you."

I shake my head. "She's never needed me. And now, all she wants is to get under my skin."

"Is it getting your attention?"

I swallow, looking away from Roger. I know what he's suggesting. But I don't know how to get past her hostility. I'm not even sure I want to.

We walk to the play structure, our feet sinking in the bark. Little kids, toddlers, run around, climbing up rope ladders, crawling through tunnels, and slipping down slides. The adults watching them cast questioning looks in our direction.

"How about the swings?" I ask, pointing.

"Why? Still think you can beat me?" Roger challenges, raising his brows.

I stare up at his tall, skinny frame, his coarse, home-cut dark hair, that familiar smile. Feeling a sudden pang in my chest, warm and strong.

Then I'm running, Roger right behind me. I jump onto the swing and pump my legs as fast as I can to get up higher, faster than he can.

We're flying, taking turns touching the sky with our toes as we hit the highest point in our swing.

"Still too slow," Roger remarks, a smirk tucked into his cheek as we lose altitude, settling into a gentle glide.

"I almost had you this time," I shoot back.

"Whatever helps you sleep at night, Nina."

The closer we come back down to the ground, the more I feel the weight of my disappointments settling on my shoulders once again.

"Do you ever think that things should happen a certain way?" I ask suddenly. "Like it's all a linear equation? You do X, you get Y. Every single time."

Thirteen years of private lessons, auditions, competitions, music intensives . . . I worked too hard to have my future in music hanging on a waitlist.

"Yeah, I do." Roger's smile is sad. It's jarring.

We hop off the swings and head back to the path toward his car.

"Dad was young, healthy, in good shape. Yet he's not here to see me graduate."

"No." I feel my throat tighten, remembering Mr. Kishimoto's big laugh and his teriyaki chicken. "He's not."

"I get it," Roger says gently. "I wish things were linear too. Guaranteed. That my brothers could have had the chance to grow up with their dad. That my mom didn't have to struggle so much to make ends meet. That I still had my dad to lean on for advice. But sometimes you get Z when you expect Y."

"It's not right." I think of all the days after Mr. Kishimoto's funeral, when Roger was just a shadow of himself. Helping his mom take care of his little brothers. Still showing up to youth group events, but sometimes bursting into tears or asking for hugs. Unafraid to talk it out, to grieve openly.

"But it is what it is," Roger says as we climb back into his car.

"And you're fine with that?" I press.

Roger exhales, pulling out of the parking lot and onto the street. "I guess for me, it's more about each moment now than a specific outcome. The people I choose to be with, the person I am."

I wish I could accept, move on, the way Roger's moved on. But instead, I keep circling these same trees in the same woods. Looking for Y, when there's only Z—Carmen's dismissal, getting second chair, losing my lead role, being waitlisted.

When Ethan jumped and I shattered.

41

I'M FLIPPING THROUGH the hanging garment bags in my closet, one after another after another. But I'm not seeing my dress. I *need* my dress.

It's your BIG DAY!!!!! Roger had texted earlier. **You got this, Nina.**

I had felt a flash of warmth knowing he was going to be at my senior recital, rooting for me. But now, as I get ready, I feel my throat tightening, a pounding in my chest.

I rush downstairs where Dad stands by the front door, his car keys in hand and suit jacket draped over his arm.

"Did Mom take my dress?"

"I'll ask," Dad frowns, reaching for his phone. "But we really need to leave, Nina."

"I know, I know." I head back upstairs and rifle back through the hanging garment bags holding all the other dresses from all my other performances over the years. Every dress except for the one I need now.

"She says it's in the back right-hand side of your closet," Dad calls from the foyer.

"No, it's not!" I shout back. I can't believe I was so hung up about the missing straps. Now I don't even have the dress.

I duck under my bed, yank out my dresser drawers, and

tip over my trash can. The seconds add up to minutes. This is not happening, not happening—

"Cleaning your room?"

Carmen stands in my doorway in black pants and a striped button-up shirt. Her makeup is light, neutral, her short hair combed and parted, the black roots stark against the bleached blond ends. It's strange to see her in real clothes looking almost pulled together for the first time in months.

Especially since she had told Mom she wasn't coming.

"My dress!" I pounce on the black garment bag in her hands. "I've been looking for it everywhere."

"Well," she shrugs like she couldn't care less. "Now you have it."

I stare hard into her red-rimmed eyes, wondering what kind of game she's playing. I've been looking for an opportunity to press in, ask questions, like Roger suggested. But right now, there isn't time.

Sitting in the back seat of Dad's car, I close my eyes and try to go through my visualization routine, the mental rehearsal of my recital from beginning to end. But Carmen's messing with Dad's stereo settings, Mom's texting, asking for my ETA, and everything that needs to happen in the next twenty-five minutes is crashing through my head.

"I told you to get here at six!" Mom flies out the back door of the performance hall as we pull up. With her fitted light gray dress and matching heels and her freshly dyed hair swept in an updo, she looks almost regal. The result of hours of primping and preparing for Grandma's inspection. "People are starting to arrive and you're not even dressed—"

Her voice breaks off as she catches sight of Carmen in the front passenger seat. "Carmen?" she says, her eyes widening.

In her head, I can almost see the script changing, the lines rewritten from explaining Carmen's absence, to explaining why she looks the way she does now.

"We're going to find parking," Dad calls, pulling away from the curb.

Mom rushes me down a series of hallways and into a small back room.

My stomach knots at the sight of Mom's curling iron heating on the wide dressing room table and her collection of expensive makeup bottles and brushes.

"I already did my hair and makeup," I say. I didn't think I needed to state the obvious, but she pushes me down into a chair and hands me a pack of makeup wipes.

"Are you even using heat protectant?" Mom parts and sections my hair, grimacing as if my split ends offend her. "Your hair is so dry . . . and your *skin*!" Mom tsks. "You really need to start taking omega-3 supplements."

"I *do* take them." I try to keep my voice neutral, but the knot in my stomach only cinches tighter.

"Every day?"

I bite back a response. Checking instead the notifications on my phone, the number of times the streaming link to my performance was shared. But even those stats aren't satisfying.

A loud rap on the door.

"Come in," Mom replies.

A man in a ball cap and headset cracks the door. "We need Nina for the sound check."

"Now?" Mom continues to dispense organic styling spray on my hair in alarming quantities.

"We're at a quarter till."

Mom glances at her watch and then at my face. I see her weigh the possibility of completing a full makeover in the next forty-five seconds.

I don't take that chance. Tossing the unopened package of makeup wipes on the table, I jump out of the chair and grab my violin case.

"Nina, you still need to change—"

"I'll do it later!" I lunge for the door, dodging Mom's critical gaze. I don't need her probing questions, her commentary about my body while I'm getting dressed.

"Make sure you reapply your mineral powder and lipstick," Mom calls. "Straighten your posture. Use the restroom before—"

The door claps shut behind me.

I hear the dull hum of voices in the lobby and catch glimpses of the dessert table, the decorations, the display of my music awards. I recognize Mrs. Kishimoto's artistic touch in all the details.

"Your accompanist is here." The sound tech ushers me backstage. "Feel free to warm up as you normally would. We'll be making some adjustments to the equipment, optimize the sound."

I run through some scales, then practice a couple passages with the accompanist. My fingers feel cold, stiff.

"Okay. We're done here. Show starts in five."

The dressing room is empty. I lock the door behind me and quickly zip on my dress and step into my heels. But something feels different.

Looking in the mirror, I see thin blue straps breaking up the expanse of my shoulders. Straps cut from another dress—almost, but not quite, the right blue. I finger the small hand stitches, hidden, on the backside of the fabric. It doesn't make sense. Who would do this? Certainly not—

The timer on my phone beeps. Two minutes left.

I check my makeup, reapply deodorant, and start my breathing exercises. But when I close my eyes, I remember another blue dress, another black-tie event. Ethan and I making faces, taking photos, our expressions mutating from one shot to the next. The walk across the parking lot, that kiss—

Zero minutes. Time to head out.

"Rich, you need to take care of this." Dad paces the narrow hall outside the dressing room, his phone pressed to his ear. "I already told you. I'm not coming into the office tonight."

There is a new impatience in his voice. "Yes, I'm at Nina's recital. We're all here and it's starting now." He rubs his hand over his face, the bags under his eyes more prominent than I remember. "Fine. Text me if you have questions. Don't call." A long pause. "I'm sorry, Rich. I really need to go."

I retrace my steps backstage, my heels clicking against the tile floor. Someone hands me a bottle of water as I mount the stairs. I take a sip, but my throat's still dry.

On the other side of the curtain, applause ripples as Mr. Bergamaschi finishes his introduction and steps away from the mic.

My accompanist appears beside me. Somehow, I'm holding my bow and violin. I really need to pee, but there's no time and the curtain is parting and I'm walking to center stage.

It doesn't seem to matter how many times I've made this walk. On other nights, on other stages, in front of other crowds or panels of judges. I still feel the same tightness in my stomach, hear the same affirming mantra—*don't screw up*—in my head.

As if from a distance, I hear my accompanist play the opening chords to the first movement of the Bartók concerto. I take a breath, lifting my violin to my chin and positioning my bow.

I begin to play, my fingers moving along the fingerboard of my violin, my bow pulling and tugging against the strings. Every movement practiced, mechanical.

I'm reaching for that moment where the tangle of my thoughts unravel. Where the stage, the lights, the audience—everything fades and I can only hear the music, its sweetness and power. Feel that unbearable ache of drawing it forth and pouring it out. No thoughts, only emotion.

But the stage, the audience, the lights, everything stays sharp, real. I'm moving through the piece, but the piece is not moving me. Every note falling flat, dull.

On the far-right side of the auditorium, Dad sits with his chin in his hand, frowning at a message on his phone. In the center section, Roger and Mrs. Kishimoto wrestle Roger's little brothers back into their seats. Roger pointing toward the stage as if to say "Pay attention." My seven cousins sit together on the left side of the auditorium. I see them leaning in to whisper to each other. Mr. Bergamaschi in the front row shakes his head, motioning for me to "make it come alive."

I'm trying, but I can't.

Up front, Grandma and my aunts and uncles sit with Mom and Mr. Bergamaschi. But there's something strange about their expressions. Like they've seen something shocking, something unexpected.

I look at Mom, her hands clenched, jaw flexed, body angled away, and I immediately think of Carmen.

Where is she anyway?

A hot, gusty anger rises up in me. I should have known she showed up just long enough to make a scene. On *my* day, *my* event—

I feel my breath catch.

I see her. Carmen. Standing alone by the back doors of the auditorium, her arms folded across her chest, looking directly at me. Just listening.

Something tightens in my throat. The hot gust of anger falters. Was I wrong? Could she really be here for me, knowing she'd be scrutinized, knowing she'd disappoint?

I'm half-listening to the accompaniment solo, counting the measures before I come in. Five measures. Four.

Flipping through my head is a catalogue of every formal dress I've seen Carmen wear: proms, graduation, piano recitals, weddings. Dress after dress after dress.

Three measures, two measures, one—

The volleyball banquet, Carmen's senior year.

The dress she wore when she was named MVP. The one she cut to fix mine.

Don't think, Ethan had told me once. *Just do.*

I swallow hard as everything fades and all I hear is the music.

42

APPLAUSE. LONG AND loud, pressing against me like a wall, a wave.

I'm breathing hard, the final note of the second movement reverberating in my chest. There is a numbness in my fingertips, a sheen of sweat against my neck.

I wish I could stay in this space. No thoughts, no sense of time, just emotion and eternity.

But already, the stage, the lights—everything sharpens, coming back into focus. I see Mr. Bergamaschi nod, catch Mrs. Kishimoto's smile and Roger's fist pump. I feel Grandma's weighted gaze, her grudging acknowledgment. So hard to come by.

I've wanted this moment more than anything.

Looking past their faces, I search the back of the auditorium where Carmen had stood, listening. A different Carmen, more like the old, less like the new. The Carmen who cut her dress to fix mine.

She isn't there.

Something sinks in my chest. As I walk backstage for intermission, my phone buzzes, Mom summoning me to the refreshments area to socialize.

It's intermission, I want to text back. *My space, my time.*

Not to mention, I have the third movement of the Bartók concerto to prepare for.

I use the bathroom and then check my makeup in the mirror, smoothing my hair back behind my ears.

Above me, voices filter in through the open vent windows. "—they need a decision from us tonight. Vin, you *have* to call the Gallagher rep back before—"

I recognize that agitated staccato. But this time it's not a voice on the other end of Dad's phone. It's Rich Bashir, here, at my recital.

"Rich, did you see this email?" Dad interjects, his voice sharp, cold. "This is the second contract we've lost in the last four weeks. One you were supposed to secure."

"I have, I *am*. But no one's taking my calls or answering my emails. I'm doing everything I can—"

"No. You're not," Dad says, and I can almost see him pressing his fingers to his temples, pinching the bridge of his nose. "You haven't been there for the audits, the restructuring, the layoffs. We need additional funding, which you haven't come through with either. Yet you show up *here*? *Now*? Bothering me about a contract we already lost?"

"I didn't know we lost it. Look, Vin, you don't understand how difficult things—"

"That's enough," Dad snaps. "I don't want to talk about this tonight. Go home, Rich."

"I came to see your family. Support Nina's big performance," Rich wheedles, his voice losing the defensive tone. "I don't know why you never invite me to these events. I've practically seen these girls grow up and now you cut me out. It's like my divorce all over—"

Their voices fade as I push open the bathroom door and walk down the hall toward the lobby.

"Nina!" Lucy rushes up. "That was phenomenal. I. Had. Chills. Just ask Roger."

I don't want to ask Roger how he knows that. In fact, I suddenly can't *stand* seeing the two of them together.

"I knew you'd do a great job, Nina." Roger smiles down at me, his dark eyes crinkling. In a button-down shirt and pressed navy pants, he looks strangely dapper. I want to make a crack, asking if he couldn't find his Kirkland khaki shorts.

"Nina."

An uncompromising grip closes above my elbow. I recognize Grandma's gold and jade rings, her suffocating perfume.

"Your mother is looking for you." Sparing a tight nod at Lucy and Roger, Grandma steers me toward the refreshments table, her pace almost urgent.

"It's a shame, really, what Carmen has done to herself." Her loud whisper grates in my ear. I feel almost nauseous at the severity of her judgment.

"You don't know what she's going through," I rush to say before thinking.

"Her volleyball scholarship, her science major and business minor, thrown away. She used to be so beautiful and look what she's done to her face, her hair. Such a waste." Grandma tsks.

"It's *not* a waste—"

"Nina! There you are," Aunt Vivian's voice booms. "What a performance!"

Uncle Nelson starts slapping his hands together, clapping alone until everyone else joins in.

Heat crawls up my neck and onto my face as I stand in front of my aunts and uncles and cousins. A formidable group, done up and dressed up tonight in their Armani, Fendi, Versace, and Louis Vuitton.

"I keep telling Wendy and Owen to practice, practice, practice their flute and cello," Aunt Vivian continues, nudging my cousins. "But they just want to play Nintendo and watch anime."

Wendy rolls her eyes then stares back down at her phone.

"But of course they are top of their class," Aunt Vivian says airily. "In just a couple years they will be where you are, getting ready to head off to a good college."

"Right," I manage, my face getting warmer, the bodice of my dress cinching tight, tighter.

"Your mom told us you applied to twelve schools," Uncle Edward says. "I'm sure it's difficult to make a decision."

"Of course it is." Grandma pins me with her weighty gaze.

"Actually," I begin, and out of the corner of my eye, I see Mom shake her head. But I'm tired of trying to bench press the bar of their expectations. "It's not a hard decision because I only got admitted to one school and I'm waitlisted at another."

"What?" Aunt Kate frowns and Uncle Nelson looks confused. Grandma's lips tighten.

"How can that be possible?" Uncle Alex asks. "You have so much talent, Nina."

"Anything is possible," Aunt Vivian says. "Just look what happened to Carmen. All those schools offering sports scholarships. She could have gone anywhere, but now—"

"Tell us, Nina. What happened to Carmen?" Uncle Edward prods. "A change like that didn't happen overnight. It's positively shocking."

They're pressing in with their cups of punch and plates of tiramisu. Fishing for answers, details they can salivate over, dissect on their long car ride home.

My phone buzzes in my hand, an incoming call. I pick up, not caring who it is.

"Hi!" I speed walk through the lobby and out the front doors of the performance hall. I know I should be going in the opposite direction, preparing for the third movement of the Bartók concerto. But what I really need is some air.

"Nina?"

I frown, pulling the phone from my ear. It's an unknown number but the voice sounds just like Bea.

"Bea?" I ask, my tone guarded.

"Where are you?" Her words sound forced, rushed.

"The old theater at the university. Why?"

"Good," she exhales. "We're at the right place. Come outside. Do you see Jayden's car?"

"What?" I head toward the street, searching in the quickly fading sunlight for an old white Saturn. "Why are you here? What's going on?"

A car door opens and Bea steps out onto the sidewalk, waving me over. "Let's go, Nina!" she urges.

"Go *where*?" I glance back at the building. "I need to finish my recital."

"I know," Bea snaps. "That's how we found your location. Your livestream."

"We came from Danny's." Jayden grips the steering wheel, his brow furrowed and jaw tense.

"Danny's," I repeat. I know that name from somewhere, but I can't quite place it.

"Get in," Bea orders.

"I—What? No!" I stumble back a step.

Bea grabs me by the shoulders. "We need to find your sister. Now."

"My sister?" I shake my head, not getting it.

"Carmen." Bea yanks open the back door of Jayden's car and pushes me in. "She showed up at Danny's house about ten minutes ago, cleared out his stash, and took off in his car."

Words, words, words coming at me like flash grenades. I fumble with the seat belt, my ears ringing.

Jayden waits for Bea to get in, then accelerates toward the intersection. "She wouldn't tell us anything. Just walked in and out."

"We've tried texting her and calling her. But she's not picking up. We think she may be OD'ing somewhere." Bea twists around in her seat, her kohl-lined eyes boring into mine. "I need you to tell me where, Nina."

Like I would know. Like I'm supposed to know. How am I supposed to know?

The seat belt is an iron band across my chest, my dress a vise. I feel each breath, hot and shallow. *Not real*, I tell myself. *Not real.*

"If Ethan were here, he'd talk her down, talk her out of it." Bea's voice softens. "He was always her person."

Her person.

The words hit me with a sudden, rocking jolt.

Bea keeps talking, but my mind is reeling, splintering. All the times I wondered whether Ethan and I were "complicated," whether things would have worked out if I were more like Carmen, less like me. The *someone else*—

"Call."

Jayden's voice. I hear it, but it seems fuzzy, distant, as my mind spins back, back to last October, to Carmen's contact pulled up on my phone. Wanting to tell her I met someone, imagining her voice on the other end of the line saying "So, tell me. Is he *fire?*"

I didn't call her then and I didn't call her later, when Ethan jumped and I—

I'm shattering—

"Call. Her."

The fuzziness dissipates and suddenly I can hear everything. Dogs barking, a car alarm blaring, in the distance, a train whistle—

I clap a hand over my mouth, holding back a scream. I can't do this, can't *do* this—

Bea snatches my phone, dials, and shoves the phone back at me.

"She's not going to answer," I wail.

"Shut up." Bea says, but her voice is hoarse, hollow. "She needs you."

The call is ringing, ringing out, my body shaking, shattering. I should have called her back in October and all the months after. Even if she didn't pick up, I could have tried.

"Nina?"

I latch onto Carmen's voice like a life preserver. "Where *are* you?" I hear fear in my voice, desperation. "Please tell me."

"I was"—Carmen's voice is faint, slow, as if needing to fish each word from a bucket of letters—"was going to stay . . .

for your whole recital. But then . . . he showed up . . ." Her slurred words trail off.

"Who—" I begin.

The call cuts out. It's over, done. Just like that.

But I heard it. Just as she ended the call. Axles grinding, steel wheels screaming along steel tracks. I'd know that sound anywhere. Still hear it in my dreams.

"She's by the tracks," I whisper.

"Which ones?" Jayden shouts.

Tears spring to my eyes. I shake my head, afraid to answer. Afraid I'll be wrong and it will be my fault.

"Which ones do you think?" Bea screams, answering for me as she dials 911.

43

SIRENS WAILING, VOICES shouting, lights flashing. Carmen's body slumped against the steep embankment by the railroad tracks, lips blue, no pulse.

Chest compressions. A defibrillator. Another series of chest compressions. The paramedics trying to restart her heart. But she isn't coming out of it. Not coming out of it . . .

I scream her name over and over. Like it's going to bring her back.

Carmen's body loaded on a stretcher. Limbs loose, feet somehow bare.

I search the embankment for her shoes, but before I can find them, the ambulance doors slam shut.

I collapse onto the gravel embankment, my hands pressed to my chest. I rock back and forth, back and forth on my knees.

Not real.

The two words that kept the truth just far enough away so I could function, carry on. Continue the pretense that loss couldn't touch me, grief couldn't break me.

But it can. It has. It does. And here it is, all over again.

Please, no. Not Carmen too.

The squeal of tires. My parents jumping out of the car,

running up the embankment. Blue lights, red lights, staining the night sky. The police questioning Jayden and Bea.

I stare at the white cross bearing Ethan's name. The flowers lying beside it.

Mom's roses.

44

BREATH. THE SUBTLE rise and fall of the chest. Oxygen in, carbon dioxide out.

In and out. In and out.

A seamless cycle, until it's not.

Beige walls, tile floor, plastic chairs. It doesn't matter if I'm standing, sitting, pacing, or dozing, I see only the erratic lines of the cardiac monitor and hear the harsh thump and hiss of the ventilator.

It's hard to believe it's already the next morning.

I close my eyes, thinking of Carmen standing by the back doors of the auditorium, her arms folded across her chest, looking directly at me. Just listening.

It meant so much to have her there.

On the other side of the room, my parents' faces alternate between pain and disbelief. Dad, sitting in silence, his head in his hands. Mom looking up medical terms on her phone, badgering the nurses, the doctors for an update. Nothing exists outside these hospital walls. There are only the blinking numbers, the glowing lights, the draining bags of fluid. Evidence of life, of hope. Hope that somehow, someway, Carmen will live.

My phone buzzes. It's Bea calling, wanting the latest.

I step out into the hall and look for someplace quiet,

perhaps a corner by a potted tree. It's a relief to walk out of that room with its beige walls and plastic chairs.

"Carmen's still out," I tell Bea. "They're monitoring her vitals. But the doctors haven't said anything one way or the other." A fact that is driving my mom crazy, but I leave that part out.

"So, they'll take her off the ventilator when she wakes up?" Bea asks.

"*If*," I correct, the knot in my stomach tightening.

"She's strong," Bea assures me. "She'll make it."

"Sure." It's strange talking without the hostility between us. Stranger still to accept that Bea knows Carmen in ways that I don't. "You could have told me, you know. About them."

Carmen and Ethan. Ethan and Carmen. Doesn't matter which way I spin it, part of me still doesn't quite believe, doesn't quite accept.

"You're right," she says, after a beat. "I'm sorry."

I draw in a sharp breath, remembering the sudden, rocking jolt of Bea's words. *Her person.* She'd told me there was someone else, but I never imagined it'd be Carmen.

"So, how'd they meet?"

"At Danny's a couple years ago."

"Her senior year," I say, mostly to myself.

"She first showed up at his place, then started coming to our other house parties. She'd drink, take some hits, but she mostly wanted pills. It was weird. She didn't seem like the type. Too perfect, you know?"

"I know." I'd grown up in the shadow of her perfection.

Her vanishing act the start of senior year. Closing herself off to me slowly, deliberately. Only to open herself to someone else—Ethan.

Ethan would still be here today, Katheryn had told me, *if it weren't for people like you.*

Someone *like* me. Someone who also spent time around Ethan. Hung out in his room, attended his events. Someone she would have met.

Carmen.

I suck in a sharp breath.

"So, what happened?" Bea presses. "What triggered her to go to Danny's and then to the tracks?"

Immediately, I think of her fall from Grandma's pedestal. But it was more than that.

My chest aches as I recall her slurred words over the phone.

I was—was going to stay . . . for your whole recital. But then . . . he showed up . . .

Who showed up?

I scour my memories. Rich's voice filtering in through the vent windows of the bathroom. The one unexpected guest at my recital, only because Dad didn't invite him this time. But he was still a family friend, certainly not someone who could have triggered Carmen—

"Nina?" I turn as Mom rounds the corner in her fitted light gray dress, her matching heels ringing against the tile.

"That's my mom," I tell Bea. "I have to go."

"Okay, talk later," Bea says, and we end the call.

"Nina." Mom frowns, planting herself directly in front of me. "I've been looking all over for you. Mrs. Kishimoto's here to take you home."

"Home?" I try to step around her to get back to Carmen's room. "But I'm staying here."

"No." Mom's tired gaze flicks from my face to my recital

dress, lingering on the sewed-on straps that are almost but not quite the right blue, as if noticing them for the first time. "Go home. Change. Get some sleep."

I look down at the creased blue satin, the stained skirt, the torn hem. It seems like some other girl wore this dress on a different night, a different stage.

"But what if—" I swallow hard, afraid to say it. As if saying it would make it true. "What if Carmen—"

"She'll be fine." The certainty in Mom's voice conflicts with her frantic questioning of the nurses, the doctors, ever since we arrived.

"Fine?" My breath quickens, unable to accept her answer. Needing to push back this time. "How can you say that?" My voice rises, turning heads now in the waiting room. "She hasn't *been* fine. Not now. Not before."

Mom shakes her head and reaches for her phone. But there's no incoming call, no new text message. It's just me. Just her.

"Leave, Nina."

My chin trembles as I step past her, turning left to the elevators instead of taking a right to Carmen's room. The metal doors clang shut and the elevator takes me down, down, down to the first floor where, just outside the automatic sliding glass doors, Mrs. Kishimoto waits. Her green minivan idling at the curb.

45

IT'S DUSK WHEN I finally wake, the sky fading from pink and orange to indigo. Lights shine in windows up and down our street, warm and inviting.

But not here. Our house is empty, silent, dark.

Carmen's last words to me over the phone run through my head, unbidden.

. . . he showed up.

When Mrs. Kishimoto dropped me off earlier this morning, I went through the entire guest list for my senior recital. Making notes next to people Carmen may not have liked. But no one stood out.

I check my phone, but there aren't any updates from my parents. Only a missed call and two text messages from Roger.

Heard about Carmen.

A crying face emoticon.

Do you want company?

Yes. No. I don't know. I suddenly realize, tonight is senior prom. Would he really miss that to hang out here with me?

I grab fresh clothes from my closet and head to the bathroom to wash my hair, brush my teeth, and do something with my face. I'm part way through blow-drying my hair when I realize I'm just going through the motions, following my routine. Who cares what I look like when Carmen is in the hospital, her life hanging in the balance?

Not real.

I switch off the blow-dryer and stare at Carmen's toiletries scattered over our shared bathroom counter, feeling a lump swell in my throat.

My mantra, my routines, my goals, they're all blinders I keep reaching for like I can make myself untouchable. Above working through the devastation of loss, reaching out to others, admitting I need help. Just like Mom.

Help.

I. Need. Help.

Even now, I can't bring myself to say it out loud to an empty room, an empty house. As if these spaces would judge me, mock me for my weakness.

I head downstairs, hitting all the light switches as I go to make the house feel brighter, warmer.

The phone rings. Dad's business line in his office downstairs. Nobody but Dad takes calls from that line, but I pick up anyway.

"Vin!" The voice on the other end of the line is tight, vibrating with energy. I don't recognize it. "*Finally*. I've been trying to reach you—"

"This isn't Vin," I say, interrupting. "It's his daughter, Nina."

A long pause. "This is Philip. I work with your dad. Is he home?" His words are clipped, urgent.

"He's . . . busy right now," I answer. "But I can take a message."

"Tell him to call me back as soon as possible," Philip says in the same clipped tone. "We've had a team of auditors looking over our books and they've finally tracked down a leak he will be *very* interested in."

A leak. Vaguely, I remember Dad on the phone with Philip the day Carmen arrived home unannounced. Something about unapproved travel expenses: airfare, hotels, meals—

"What would he be interested in?" I ask, probing.

Another long pause. "The undocumented travel expenses," Philip finally says. "They've been traced back to Rich Bashir. Remember. Tell him to *call me.*"

"Okay," I hear myself say, but it doesn't make sense to me. Rich has been invested in Dad's startup since it was just a name and a patent. He even had me believing in its growth, its success. Why would he do something to jeopardize that?

I feel unsettled as I head to the kitchen and take Mrs. Kishimoto's enchilada casserole out of the fridge. I cut a small square and heat it up, then pour myself a glass of water.

I sit at the dining table, picking at the casserole. Mrs. Kishimoto always makes this dish too spicy. I can feel the heat now in my nose, tearing up my eyes. But I keep eating, keep shoveling the food down, bite after bite. Even though my mouth is on fire and tears sting my eyes. Afraid that the moment I'm not doing something normal, tangible, I'm going to start screaming and I won't stop.

In my head, I see the blank monitor in Mr. Kishimoto's hospital room after he died. The numbers erased and the display reset to the program's main menu.

I remember now how everyone in the room lined up, taking their turn to touch his hands, his face, and say their last goodbyes.

But not me. I had stood off to the side, staring at the

blank monitor like it was all up to me. That if only I stared long enough, hard enough, the numbers and colored lines would reappear and we could all stop shattering on the inside.

But it wasn't up to me. Not then, not now, not *ever*.

My muscles clench, my fingers tightening around my water glass. I look out at the immaculate kitchen, every crumb swept, every countertop wiped, and every dish put away. Just how Mom keeps it, like she's the one staring at the blank monitor and everything is all up to her.

I jump at the sound of a splintering crash, my water glass hitting the corner of the kitchen island.

For a second, I don't believe it. That *I* threw it. Me.

I stare at the mark on the white marble countertop, the jagged pieces of glass scattered across the floor, the spray of water against the island. I assess the mess. And it is a mess, an ugly, ugly mess.

My stomach twists at the thought of Mom walking in and seeing this. I can almost hear her key in the lock, the front door opening—

And so what? So what if she does see? Why can't I, like Roger, just take my chances?

But I'm too well-trained. Trained to sweep and hide and pretend that nothing ever happened here. So, I get down on my hands and knees and pick up the shards of glass and toss them into a brown paper sack.

There are pieces everywhere. My socks are wet, my fingertips bleed, and at senior prom tonight, they are playing everything from the classics to the latest K-pop hits.

The dance floor will be packed. People dancing in pairs, in groups. Even the solo dancer doing his own shuffle on the sidelines isn't alone. People are shouting, whistling, pushing to join in.

I should be there in a metallic gold dress and matching heels, my hand on Ethan's arm, his corsage around my wrist. I've pictured it a hundred times, from the cut of his tux to the way it'd feel to slow dance in his arms. I can almost catch the light, clean scent of his cologne, feel his hazel eyes on mine, see the smile playing across his perfect lips.

But he isn't here and he isn't mine.

Her person.

Did Carmen know of Ethan's pain? Did she know where he was headed that night, what he was going to do?

See you tomorrow?

The text I sent Ethan the night I got home from YMI.

Yeah, he had responded. And I'd believed him. Stupid. I'm so, so stupid.

I mash my fist into the tile floor, feeling the sharp prick of glass, the sting, the pain. I see the blood, bright red against the white tile. I push down hard, wanting it to hurt. Not just from the inside, but on the outside this time.

The empty pill bottles, the needles, the box of fentanyl patches next to Carmen's unresponsive body. Out in the open, as if condemning me for my silence.

And maybe I knew.

Maybe it was why I reached for my blinders, kept reaching for my blinders. Because if I didn't really see it, acknowledge it, I wouldn't have to say a thing.

46

SHE'S AWAKE.

I reread Dad's text, ten, twenty times on the way to the hospital with Mrs. Kishimoto. I'm afraid to believe, to accept. As if at any moment, this lifeline would be jerked away and I'd be left to drown.

We pull up to the hospital entrance and I see the white concrete columns, the fluttering flag, the automatic sliding glass doors that now reflect the pale blue sky. Everything feels too familiar in all the wrong ways.

Biting my lip, I reach for the door handle of the car, my right hand stiff and sore from the cuts the night before.

"Thanks for the ride."

Mrs. Kishimoto offers me a small smile. Reaching over, she squeezes my left arm hard. I feel that squeeze the whole walk down to the elevators, the ride up to the general floor. Wonder.

Why the smile, the squeeze? Does she know something I don't? Was she trying to prepare me?

She's awake.

Awake is good, right? I'd jumped to that conclusion, but what if that was all she was? Awake and . . . not much else. What if the question now was not between life and death, but levels of physical and mental disability? What would that mean for her, for us? How would that change—

"I don't *want* to be here!"

Carmen's voice, hoarse and punctuated, hits me right in the chest as I exit the elevator.

Her new room is just a few steps away, the door standing open.

"You don't know what you're saying," I hear Mom retort, her voice harried, sharp. "Get some rest. You're not yourself."

Why are you arguing with her? I want to shout at my mom. *Carmen's speaking, she's alive. Isn't that enough?*

Carmen's coarse laughter stops me just outside the door. "But I *am* myself. You just can't accept it."

"Carmen," Dad pleads. "Maybe we can talk about this—"

"Later?" Carmen scoffs. Peering in, I catch a glimpse of her sitting up in bed, eyes red rimmed, face ashy gray, a white ring around her lips. "Don't pretend like we ever talk about things that matter. You just give me money and patch things over."

Mom turns on Dad, her voice ragged. "Vin, I *told* you—"

"No." Dad holds up a hand, palm out as if to stop whatever Mom means to say. "That isn't fair, Carmen. We did talk."

"Yeah, about grades, volleyball." Carmen shrugs, picking at her sheets. I hang back in the doorway, just out of her line of sight. "But you and Mom didn't try figure out what was really wrong. You never pulled it out of me."

"Tell us." Dad takes a step toward Carmen's bed. He places a hand on the metal rail. "Please. We want to hear it."

Carmen's forehead puckers, her doubtful gaze sliding from Dad's face to Mom's to the hospital phone on the stand beside her. "No," she decides, ignoring the tangle of tubes and tape and folding her arms. "You don't. You're just saying that to get me back into my box to perform."

"Then what do you want from us?" Mom erupts, throwing her hands up.

"Melanie—" Dad's voice is a warning.

"See?" Carmen exclaims. "You're not even listening right now!" Her flashing eyes graze me as I step into the room. "You are doing to Nina *exactly* what you did to me. You don't let her screw up. You don't give her an opinion—"

"We don't need to talk about this right now," Mom huffs, crossing the room to pick a napkin off the floor, straighten the plastic water cups on the stand. As if by putting the room in order, she can fix everything.

"Mel, I think we do—" Dad begins. But his phone vibrates in his pocket, and he fumbles for it, frowning at the name on the screen. I wonder if it's Philip, still trying to reach him about the audit results.

"Everybody, just get out," Carmen orders, her face pinched, hard.

We don't move.

"I said, *get out*!" she screams.

We startle from our places, my parents bumping into each other as they head for the door.

"Come on, Nina," Mom says, her voice expectant, as if knowing I'll comply.

But I just got here. I'm not going to leave. Not yet.

"Nina," Mom repeats.

I walk toward Carmen's bed until I am so close I can hear her breathing. In and out. In and out. Her lungs this time and not the ventilator.

Carmen sits upright, her body rigid, her arms still folded. She stares at the opposite wall at a picture of a boat in a large frame, seemingly oblivious to my presence.

There are so many things that need to be said between us, about her, about me, about Ethan. I don't know where or how to start.

"You're shaking," I say after a long moment, reaching out to touch her arm. "Are you cold?"

She flinches at my touch. "No."

"Did something happen?" I press. Wondering if the outburst I walked into was triggered by something the hospital staff did or something my parents said.

She doesn't answer right away and for a second I wonder if I'm being too much. Staying when she said to go and now asking these questions.

"Did Mom or Dad tell anyone I'm here?" Carmen finally asks, her voice low and gaze focused straight ahead.

"Only the Kishimotos—" I begin.

"Then how did Rich know to call *here*?" Carmen's voice cracks. A violent shudder ripples through her body.

Rich again. His name seems to be coming up everywhere.

"I don't know," I say carefully. Maybe Dad had said something, though I doubt it based on the conversation I'd overheard between him and Rich at my recital.

Carmen falls back against her pillows and throws an arm up to cover her eyes. "Do me a favor, okay? Watch the door for me."

I glance quickly behind me, but there's no one there.

"Who am I looking for?"

"Just..." Carmen heaves a sigh. "Watch."

"Okay," I say, turning toward the door.

Behind me, I hear the mattress creak as she rolls to her side, shifting until she finds a semi-comfortable position.

I watch the door, knowing there's nowhere else I'd rather be than here, beside her. Listening to her breathe, holding on to the knowledge that she's alive.

47

IT'S STRANGE EATING out of Chinese take-out boxes at the kitchen island instead of sitting down at the glass dining table to a home-cooked meal. Everything tastes a little too salty, a little too greasy. I'm full after a few bites.

Mom gets up to pour herself a glass of water. I watch her carefully, but she doesn't seem to notice that one of the glasses is missing in the cupboard. Or that there's a mark on the corner of the kitchen island I haven't quite been able to rub out.

After dinner, I head upstairs to study. Finals week is coming up and everyone says the physics final is almost impossible to pass. But I can't focus. The words in my textbook are meaningless. I feel like I need to go somewhere, do something. But I don't know where or what.

The door to my parents' bedroom is cracked and I hear them talking about Carmen. Decisions have to be made now that she's out of critical condition. But instead, they bicker, his side, her side, over whether she should go to rehab or come home.

I realize Carmen was right back at the hospital, when she said that Mom and Dad are always talking, but they don't *listen*. I slap my textbook shut, grab a light jacket from my closet, and go downstairs.

My bike is parked up against the back wall of the garage, dusty and untouched since January. There is no lock binding the wheels and frame, no hidden key in Mom's purse, because I'm not Carmen. I'm not one to push the limits, play my parents one against the other.

I check the air in the tires and wheel my bike out the side door of the garage and through the latched gate. The night air is cool, the sky a velvet blanket pinpricked with stars. In the driveway, I swing over the bike frame, my right foot finding the toe clip, my thumb and fingers wrapping loosely around the handlebars. Every motion is fluid, like I belong here.

Lights shine from windows. The neighbor's cat crosses the street, the tags on its collar jingling. I see the flicker of a TV screen. I look at the landscaped yards, the modern architecture of the homes on this street. There isn't one weedy yard, one square, cookie-cutter house. But I wonder—behind the front doors, is it all as perfect as it seems?

Flipping on my bike light, I head for the greenbelt, listening to the familiar whiz of my tires against pavement.

Hey.

I hear Ethan's voice, like he's riding beside me. Somehow, I knew I'd hear it, just this way.

Hey, yourself.

It's been a while.

I miss his voice. I miss him. Even after everything.

I know. I draw in a shaky breath. *I've been busy.*

Avoiding me?

No. I cross a roundabout, pick up the greenbelt again at the park. *Maybe. Yes.*

Because of Carmen.

I bite my lip, feeling my body tense. *You could have told me. About you and her.*

I just didn't want you to think—

That you had someone else? I finish for him, feeling the sting of tears in my eyes.

I liked you. I wanted to get to know you. His voice is pleading, earnest. I want to believe him.

You knew I was Carmen's sister, I say. *That first day we met.* It's a statement, not a question.

Yes.

Yet you still led me on.

It was complicated.

Complicated. I'd always hated that term, even as I wondered if we were complicated.

She was at college, he says, after a long moment. *You were here.*

But she was your person. My chin trembles and I swipe at the tears streaking across my face. *How could you do this to her? To me?*

It was complicated.

You said that already. I pedal faster, past the soccer fields, the apartments, heading toward the intersection by the gourmet grocery store.

She had other guys.

Excuses. Excuses. Excuses. Never an apology.

I was trying, you know. To turn things around.

I grit my teeth. *All those school projects. What were they really about? Conditions of your probation?*

You wouldn't have understood.

You could have tried.

And have you leave?

I shake my head. *You're the one who left, remember? You left me.*

Silence.

I actually thought I meant something to you. But all along—I liked you, Nina.

My grip tightens on the handlebars as I cross the intersection and make a left. *You strung me along like some cheap substitute.*

A sigh. *What do you want me to say?*

I swallow hard, feeling something twist in my chest, an ache. The first day we met in the school library and all the days after. What was it that I wanted? What did I need him to say?

I love you. The three words drop, weighty and unapologetic. *I love you.* Those same three words, louder this time. *That's what I want you to say.*

I draw in a slow breath as I turn into my old neighborhood. Same big trees, same small, square, cookie-cutter houses. Even the same old dogs barking as I cruise by.

Nina.

I close my eyes. His voice is soft, familiar. So heartbreakingly familiar.

I... can't.

My world tilts. Everything shifting, sliding.

I've known it. Known it all along, this truth. But I didn't want to see, to accept. Instead, I weighed every look, every gesture, adding and subtracting, trying to balance the equation. Force the answer I wanted, the person I needed, not the one who was there.

I am sobbing now, tears streaming, nose running, my bike pulled up in our old driveway.

Time seems to slip away, the years flipping back. I can almost see the chalk drawings on the sidewalk, hear Carmen and me chanting as we skip rope. Two houses down, Mr. Kishimoto is grilling his teriyaki chicken and we're all invited—

Why do things have to change? I want to stay here, back before all the loss and pain and complications. When things were simply what they were, not what we needed them to be.

"It's okay," I hear myself whisper into the dark night, the soft stillness, my tears still falling, nose still running.

I wish more than anything that Ethan could have heard me say these words.

48

IN THE DRIVEWAY, a car horn beeps.

I walk past Carmen's empty room, down the stairs, and out the door to where Roger waits for me.

"You okay?" he asks as soon as I get in the car. Hearing his voice unravels something inside of me. "I was worried when I didn't hear back from you all weekend."

His missed call and text messages on Saturday asking if I needed company. I never did answer those.

"I'm sorry," I say, biting my lip, wishing he knew how much I meant it. "I figured you and Lucy were at prom. I . . . didn't want to bother you."

"Nina." Roger looks over at me, his lips turned down and his dark eyes sad.

"Roger," I say, my response automatic.

"Nina."

"Yes?"

"You are *never* a bother."

I turn away, blinking quickly, but a tear still slips down my cheek. How can he say that when I cut him out of my life last fall? When I've been cold and distant and not a little ungrateful?

His text messages in all caps followed by a string of exclamation points. The car rides to and from school. Skipping first period to walk with me in the park. I can still picture the worry in his eyes as he pushed through the crowds that morning after Ethan jumped. I have always been able to look over and find him there, just like I wished for all those years ago at the community pool.

"I'm scared," I finally say, and my voice shakes. For a second, I almost reach out to grab his hand.

When I close my eyes at night, I still hear the wail of sirens, voices shouting. Still see red lights, blue lights, Carmen's body slumped against the steep embankment by the railroad tracks.

"My parents are driving Carmen down to a women's rehab center in San Luis Obispo." I stare down at the cuts on my right hand, itchy now with scabs. "She's getting checked into a ninety-day program. The first three weeks are a blackout period. No calls, no texts, no mail." I draw in a breath. "It feels like we just got her back and now we're losing her all over again."

Roger nods, his eyes pained.

"I failed her," I say, my voice harsh.

"What do you mean?" Roger pulls into a parking space and turns off the ignition.

"I should have pressed in, tried to understand what was happening. Like you said, she needed me." But instead, I kept my blinders on as Carmen floundered, resented her for failing, falling. She fixed my recital dress and I didn't even thank her for it.

Help.

I. Need. Help.

Words I couldn't bring myself to say aloud to an empty room, an empty house.

Had Carmen been shouting them too? As we passed silently in the halls, the bathroom, the kitchen? Going about our separate lives wrapped up in our own thoughts, our own pain. Faulty in our assumptions about each other.

"You're here for her now. That's what matters."

"But none of this would have happened if I'd tried!" I shout, punching my fist against the plastic-wrapped seat.

"Nina," Roger says, and his voice is kind, so achingly kind. "You don't know that."

I shake my head, *No, not true.* But of course, Roger plows on. He could never take a hint.

"There's no changing what's happened," Roger says, undeterred. "You can only choose what you do next."

49

IT'S FINALS WEEK and though yearbooks are out and graduation is around the corner, the campus feels quieter than normal, everyone tense, focused.

Every day, when I leave for school, Mom isn't dressed for work. She's still in her pajamas when I get home, her face devoid of makeup and her hair mussed.

Yeungs always look presentable. One of Mom's Basic Rules. And I've never seen her look anything but presentable.

For the first time, I notice weeds in the front yard, dust on the piano and the charred wood coffee table.

Dad's at the office every night, handling another wave of unplanned layoffs with Philip. He'd confronted Rich about the audit findings—seven unapproved trips down to LA. Only to have Rich lash back, saying they were for business, the connections he had with his alma mater, USC. They were last-minute opportunities, and he didn't have the time to go through the approval process.

I keep hoping to hear back from my number two music college, the one I'm waitlisted for. I know time is running out and Mom wants me to confirm my acceptance to the school on her list, but I just can't bring myself to do it.

I'm still stuck on the carousel ride, decisions coming at me for my next move, my next step.

Roger's going to San Diego State, Lucy to Princeton. Bea's heading to OSU and Jayden to the Air Force.

I should be going to music college. Any one of the three that I'd painstakingly researched for their prestige, selectivity, and notable alumni. Sure, I could have done more with my essays, and my SAT scores were not what they should have been. But my pre-screen recordings were good. I had the letter of recommendation from Mr. Martinez, not to mention my extensive music resume and my acceptance to YMI. Surely that had to be enough.

Getting in has been my one dream, the one plan, ever since I picked up my first violin, started lessons with Mr. Bergamaschi at age four. The reason I'd kept auditioning, competing, performing, everything to build the skills and resume I needed. Never imagining a different outcome.

I push open the sliding glass door that leads to the backyard. It sticks a little, as if rusty with unuse. I feel drawn out across the unswept paver patio and dried-out lawn to Mom's garden roses.

Just weeks ago, the bushes were heavy with large coral blooms, the hard-won product of Mom's labors. Months of pruning, spraying, fertilizing, keeping to a schedule. The way she keeps everything else to a schedule: lawn maintenance, house maintenance, car maintenance.

Or rather, did.

Reaching out, I touch the yellowing stems, the curled leaves sticky with aphids.

I feel a lump in my throat. Was Carmen right that day I pounded on her door, yelling at her to turn down her music? Mr. Bergamaschi was coming and I needed to practice, needed everything to be perfect. Every little thing.

Don't you get it, Nina? There's no point.

I hear her voice in my head, like we're standing back in front of her bedroom door, her face so close to mine.

Mom had me playing the piano for twelve years. Twelve years. *What's it done for me? Nothing.*

Nothing?

Couldn't be. You do *X*, you get *Y*. It's a formula, an equation. Plug in time and effort and you get results, a payout. Not zero. Not nothing.

Violin, volleyball, piano, a startup company, keeping up the house, the yard, this image. We're all working, day and night, night and day, staying up late and getting up early. Doing what we've been trained to do, expecting that payout—a promotion, a prize.

Except nothing's coming.

50

THE COLLEGE ADMISSIONS article is published in the *Davis Enterprise* with its list of graduating seniors and the colleges they have chosen to attend. My name is on the last page: Undeclared.

The fallout of declining my offer of admission to the school on Mom's list to stay on the waitlist for the music college. Only to be told they don't have a spot for me this year.

51

"IT'S PARTY TIME. Let's go, Nina."

Roger stands at my door, a small black and gold cone hat perched on his head.

"I already told you, I'm not in the mood," I answer, shoving my hands into the pockets of my white shorts. The last thing I feel like doing right now is showing up to the graduation party he's hosting for the youth group seniors. I have nothing to celebrate, everything to grieve.

"Staying in this house isn't going to change that," Roger points out. "You need people."

"People," I repeat, not even trying to mask the heavy doubt in my tone.

"Yes. Like *me*, for instance." Roger smiles. Reaching forward, he snaps a matching black and gold cone hat on my head. "Now, let's go."

It's been a long time since I've hung out at the Kishimotos' house. Everything seems smaller than I remember—the kitchen, the living room, the backyard.

"Nina, can you take the taquitos out of the oven?" Mrs. Kishimoto asks, handing me a pair of oven mitts.

"Yes." I pull on the mitts and slide the trays out from the oven and set them on the stove top. "Do you have serving platters for these?"

"The cabinet to your left, second shelf," Mrs. Kishimoto says.

I plate the Costco taquitos, laying out a row at the bottom and then neatly stacking a second and then a third layer.

"How are you doing, Nina?" Mrs. Kishimoto asks, coming up beside me and giving me a hug.

I feel my lip start to tremble, and I draw in a long breath. "Been better," I say, not really wanting to get into the details.

"Your mom worries about you," Mrs. Kishimoto says.

I shake my head. Disappointed, angry, frustrated—definitely. Worried? Not a chance. "She's concerned about Carmen, about Dad's startup, about what Grandma thinks—"

"And also, why you've stopped playing the violin. And how things ended up with the music college you wanted to attend and with the string quartet. How you've been struggling with the tragic loss of your friend and with everything that has happened to Carmen."

"She told you all that?" I ask, feeling a sudden lump in my throat, the sting of tears. All this time Mom's seen me—the *real* me.

"We talk," Mrs. Kishimoto says, pulling two boxes of Costco mini quiches from the freezer. "How about taking that taquito platter outside while I heat up these quiches?"

I nod, gripping the sides of the platter and walking carefully around the Legos and puzzles and books scattered on the floor to get to the patio door.

Outside, Lucy teeters on a ladder, putting together the black, white, and gold balloon arch kit she bought off Etsy.

"Need help?" I ask, setting the platter on a plastic folding table holding bags of chips, bowls of trail mix and popcorn, and a wide variety of canned drinks.

"Yes, actually," Lucy says, wrestling with a large white balloon. "The balloon pump is on the ground somewhere and the balloons are . . . on that folding chair."

I pick up the pump and start filling balloons, amassing a large pile around me.

"So, how'd the season end," I ask, "for the string quartet?"

Lucy glances down at me from her perch on the ladder. "We had some good gigs, but . . . it wasn't the same without you." She bites her lip. "I'm sorry. For taking over the way I did."

I shake my head. "You did what you had to." As the words leave my lips, I feel an ebbing of the anger I've been carrying ever since the anniversary party. "I'm glad you kept it going when I . . . couldn't."

Looking back, I know I was living a fantasy, thinking I could juggle it all. When I was drowning in grief, drowning under the pressure of everything coming at me.

Footsteps approach, voices talking loudly.

"What? Is that actually Nina?"

"The Catan Queen herself!"

I'm tackled from behind. The youth group is talking all at once.

"We saw your senior recital on livestream . . ."

"Heard there was some kind of family emergency . . ."

"Where are you headed this fall?"

"How have you been?"

It feels nice being in the middle of this circle. Surrounded.

Roger bursts out the patio door. "Who's ready for water balloons?" he shouts, his arms full of sloshing, black, white, and gold balloons. His little brothers tag along just behind him.

"Hey!" Lucy exclaims from her perch on the ladder. "Those are for the *balloon arch*!"

But already the water balloons are flying and exploding. My legs are wet, part of my back is wet, and there is a grass stain on my white shorts.

"Watch out, Nina!" Roger yells.

I turn just in time to see Rochelle charge around the corner lugging an enormous gold water balloon.

I run. Faster than I ever ran in PE. I dodge to the left and to the right, pushing people out of my way as Rochelle closes in.

An explosion of water. Shredded gold bits raining down. I'm drenched from head to toe.

I sputter, gasping, feeling, for a second, alive.

52

I TAKE A stack of Carmen's tattered paperbacks from her room and put them on my nightstand.

When I can't sleep, when my thoughts are spinning, dragging me down, down. When I wake with a start, hearing the scream of a train whistle or the wail of sirens, I switch on my bedside lamp and pick up a paperback.

Supernovas, hyperspace, galactic governments. I find myself flipping from one page to the next, getting pulled into very different worlds.

It's late when I hear Mom's footsteps come up the stairs and pass my bedroom door.

She's on the phone with Grandma. But she isn't painting an idealistic picture of our family, telling Grandma what she wants to hear.

"I'm not talking about Vin, I'm talking about Carmen!" Mom's voice is charged, defensive. "I *know* that. I'll get the money back to you for her car. But things are tight right now with the bills at the facility." A sigh. "Yes, Vin's trying to get things turned around at the startup. No, he can't return your funds right now. *Please*, stop asking—"

The door to my parents' room slams, but Mom's voice continues to rise.

I stare down at the tiny print on the dusty page of the

paperback in my hands, needing to get back into the story. I want to feel whatever Carmen felt as she read these same pages. Did she laugh here? Groan there? Mull over this term, that phrase?

But instead, I recall Grandma's grip closing above my elbow. I hear her loud whisper grating in my ear.

It's a shame, really, what Carmen has done to herself.

I shut my eyes and press my hands over my ears. But she's still talking, talking, in that nagging, critical voice.

Her volleyball scholarship, her science major and business minor, thrown away.

Shut up. My teeth are gritted. Carmen didn't deserve to be talked about that way. As if her only worth was when she checked all the right boxes. *Please, just shut up.*

But Grandma's voice is still in my head and it won't stop. Not now, not later.

She used to be so beautiful and look what she's done to her face, her hair. Such a waste.

A shame.

A waste.

All this time, I thought Grandma was referring to Carmen's choices, Carmen's loss. But now I'm wondering if she was speaking of her own choices, her own loss.

The down payment for Carmen's car, the seed money for Dad's startup. What else has she paid for, invested in? Expecting a payout.

Certainly not zero. Not nothing.

53

WHEN THE BLACKOUT period is over, my parents and I wait, hoping. Carmen can now send letters and make phone calls. But she doesn't write, doesn't call.

The only updates are from the care coordinator at the rehab center: Carmen still refuses to participate in group therapy, she doesn't get along with the other women, she doesn't "make an effort."

"We don't have a *choice*, Vin."

In my room, I turn up my Tchaikovsky playlist and flip to the next page of another one of Carmen's tattered paperbacks. This selection is part of a natural disaster fiction series—wind, flood, fire! But I can still hear my parents arguing. I can still feel the force of their words, the depth of their contempt.

"This is your mother's doing, isn't it?" Dad counters. "She gives her 'gifts' when everything's going the way she wants and then takes them back when they're not. Maybe she should stop calling them 'gifts' and start calling them 'loans.'"

"Whatever you call it, it's *her* money," Mom shouts. "And she wants it back. The down payment for Carmen's car, the money for your startup—"

"So, she wants to call back everything she sank into me

and Carmen? What about you and Nina?" Dad exclaims. "What about the money you took for the down payment on this house? To landscape the yard?"

"What about it?" Mom cries. "You live in this house too!"

"And those ridiculously expensive private lessons with that stuffed . . . shirt. When a college student would have been more than adequate," Dad continues. "Paying for that musician's camp in Colorado—"

"I want the best for my daughter, is that so wrong?"

"Then why'd you hold her back from going to music college? Tell the truth, Mel. You weren't so sure your mother would pay for it, right?"

"I knew she wouldn't." Mom's voice is flat, cold. "But I didn't hold Nina back either, Vin. Whatever you may say."

Tears slip down my cheeks, wetting the pages of Carmen's book.

I want the best for my daughter.

Words I thought my parents reserved only for Carmen. But all along, Mom was living them out for me too. All the long car rides to recitals, competitions, performances. Sitting in the audience whether it was on plastic chairs or plush theater seats. Cramped in the back, her arm raised, filming, when there was standing room only.

These acts I didn't even consider, didn't even acknowledge, because I was too wrapped up in my own goals, my own plans. Too blind to see the struggle as Mom tried to find the money to pay for it all.

The best.

She gave that to me. Even if it came with strings she knew she couldn't cut.

54

"THERE'S PROGRESS," CARMEN'S care coordinator informs my parents. "She's getting along better with the other residents, starting to participate in group therapy."

I linger in the kitchen where I can see my parents sitting at the glass table in the dining room, Dad's tablet open between them. Carmen's care coordinator addresses them from the screen, her tone direct and hands folded.

"There is anger. A lot of anger," Carmen's care coordinator continues. "We have her seeing a counselor two times a week."

My parents stare straight at the screen, their backs rigid, bodies angled away from each other.

"Carmen is working through it. But it's going to take time."

Time. It seems that's all there is in front of us, these days.

"Is there anything she needs?" Dad asks. "Something we can mail over?"

Carmen's care coordinator shakes her head. "No packages, no letters."

"When will she call?" Mom leans in, her hands gripping the edge of the table, her voice hungry, hoarse.

"When she's ready," she assures Mom.

"Which is—?"

"When she's ready," the care coordinator repeats.

Mom slumps back in her chair.

Nudging the tablet toward himself, Dad takes over the call, nodding and responding in all the right places as the care coordinator finishes her report-out.

Beside him, Mom's head is bowed, her shoulders shaking. I've seen her dab at her eyes, but have never seen her cry.

It breaks me.

55

"HEY." CARMEN'S VOICE is flat, devoid of clues.

It's my turn now, after weeks of Carmen speaking only to my parents. The phone calls last a minute, maybe two. Mom still talking when Carmen says she needs to go.

"Hey." I feel my body tense.

"So," she says, in that same flat voice.

The last time I saw her, I was standing beside her hospital bed, watching the door on her request as she rolled onto her side, fell asleep.

I remember listening to her breathe, holding on to the knowledge that she's alive. But I don't know how many iterations of Carmen have passed since then. She seems like a stranger again.

"How is it?" I finally ask.

"Rehab." Her voice is short. "You know."

Like I would. When she knows I don't.

"I never got to thank you," I say, "for the dress straps."

"It wasn't much."

"It was though. For me."

Dragging silence.

"Bea and Jayden," I begin, when Carmen doesn't say anything. "They've been asking about you."

"Have they," Carmen replies. And there is no inflection

in her voice, no suggestion that she's surprised, disturbed, moved in any way at our acquaintance.

"They were the ones who picked me up," I press on. "To look for you."

"You shouldn't have."

What was the alternative? I want to shout. *Let you die? Out by the tracks, alone?*

"I'm sorry," I say instead. "About Ethan."

In my head, I see the flicker of blue lights, red lights, staining the night sky. The small white cross, Mom's roses beside it. "I didn't know he was your—"

"Was," Carmen interjects. Her tone is abrupt, followed by a rough exhale. Already, I feel her shutting down, pulling away. "It doesn't matter now."

"Did he ever—" I swallow hard, the words sticking in my throat. I'm trying to hold Carmen here, for a moment more. "Mention me?"

I hear her breath, my breath, loud on either side of the call.

"I need to go," Carmen says suddenly, her voice sounding almost choked up, pained.

"But—" I falter, reaching.

The call's over just like that.

56

CARMEN'S NINETY-DAY PROGRAM is extended by a week, another.

"She's still processing," her care coordinator says in her mid-July report-out to my parents. "Working through some hard things. She needs more time before she's ready to share."

I both want to know yet dread to know what it is my sister has to share.

Our first in-person visit at Carmen's rehab center is the last week of July.

We arrive at the center ten minutes late, breaking one of Mom's Basic Rules.

Dad pulls into the first available parking spot. We jog to the entrance, rush through the sign-in process at the front desk, and hustle down a long hallway to the visiting room.

As we enter, a heavyset woman with blond curly hair comes toward us with a clipboard and pen. "Vincent and Melanie Yeung?"

"Yes," my parents answer, their voices tense, winded.

"Debbie Wurst, care coordinator." She smiles wide. "It's always nice to meet in person."

"Right," Mom answers distractedly, her gaze flicking across the room, looking for Carmen.

"Why don't you all take a seat?" Debbie offers, her smile intact and voice upbeat. "Make yourselves comfortable. I'll have Carmen here in just a moment."

We stay standing.

Mom twists her stud earring, her lips pressed tightly together. In a charcoal pantsuit and low heels, she's the most dressed up I've seen in weeks. Dad eyes the eclectic collection of multi-colored arm chairs and couches, as if doubtful of their ability to provide anything but gross discomfort.

On the other side of the room, two other families sit, talking in low tones. A husband with two young kids visiting his wife. A mom visiting her daughter.

It doesn't make sense that we're here. It should be some other family, any other family.

A shadow dims the doorway. Carmen enters, walks straight past us, and takes a seat in a narrow armchair by the window. She wears a pair of light-colored jeans, a plain white T-shirt. Her hair is pulled back into a stubby ponytail, a harsh line visible between her black roots and the old bleach job. Instead of contacts, she wears a pair of old glasses—square, dark-rimmed.

Mom gulps, her knuckles white as she grips her purse. Dad blinks quickly, reaching up to brush his face. We move toward Carmen, finding seats on the magenta couch and the green and orange armchairs beside her. Close, but not too close.

"Carmen." Mom leans forward on the couch, her purse in her lap like she's in the waiting room of Carmen's orthodontist for a routine appointment. "Are you eating the vegetables in the meal plan? Participating in the exercise classes? Remember, you have to wear sunscreen when you go outdoors—"

Carmen folds her arms across her chest and exhales loudly.

"Is there anything you need, Carmen?" Dad cuts in. "Your books, or snacks, or—"

"Yeah," Carmen grouches. "You can get me out of here."

There is something unsettling in her voice. Anger, volatility.

"We will," Dad assures her. Like this is all part of his plan, his play. Like he wasn't the last one dragged out of the house this morning. "As soon as they give us the green light—"

"Or perhaps even earlier," Mom presses, her hands gripping the purse in her lap. "The additional weeks might not be necessary—"

"They *are* necessary," Dad retorts. "And we will support her as long as she can benefit from more—"

"Talking?" Mom's voice rises, turning heads from across the room. "Yoga classes? Crafts? We can do all that for her at home."

"This is about your mother's money, isn't it?" Dad tosses back. "You're more worried about it than Carmen's well-being!"

Out of the corner of my eye, I see Debbie come toward us.

"And why is that, Vin?" Mom shouts, standing now. "How much money is your startup losing *every day*? How many people have you had to let go? Just give it up already!"

"Give it up?" Dad jumps to his feet, his voice incredulous. "*I* filed the patent, *I* built this company, *I*—"

"You, you, you!" Mom explodes. "What about my mother's seed money? What about me going back to work?"

"Please," Debbie steps between my parents. "Keep your voices down."

"We're in a slump," Dad admits, lowering his voice slightly. "But we're going to turn things around. Rich and I—"

"Rich?" Mom laughs, the sound sharp. "You two should have gone your separate ways a long time ago."

"Your voices," Debbie hisses, holding a finger to her lips. "There are other families—"

"Rich is a good guy," Dad insists, ignoring Debbie. "He's just going through a rough time. Not that you'd understand—"

"No!" Carmen shouts. Bolting out of her chair, she points a trembling finger at Dad. "Rich is *not* a good guy."

Dad frowns, glancing over his shoulder as if noticing the sudden silence in the room. "What are you saying, Carmen? Rich thinks the world of you."

"I wish he wouldn't think of me at all!" Carmen screams, her fists clenched, body rigid. "I wish I didn't *exist* to him. That he couldn't find me, talk to me, message me, show up randomly at my dorm, my classes—"

Dad's face is frozen, his expression blank. "*What?*"

Mom opens her mouth, but only a strangled sound escapes.

The room spins. I grip the sides of the orange armchair, a chill spreading from the pit of my stomach, a roaring sound in my ears.

"I never told anyone except for one person." Carmen turns, her gaze burning into mine.

Ethan Travvers.

Her person.

57

WHEN WE GET home, Mom locks herself in their bedroom, and Dad retreats to his office downstairs, their faces shocked, haunted, sad.

I head to the kitchen for water. But before I can reach for a glass, my stomach clenches and I feel my skin prickle.

So, it's going to be UCLA, huh?

I turn slowly, seeing Rich Bashir's tall muscular frame in pressed khaki pants and a pastel polo, sitting beside Carmen at our dining table, just months before her high school graduation. Helping himself to a second serving of Mom's stir-fried noodles, like he belonged here, with us.

"Go Bruins," Carmen had shot back. And I'd envied her then, the easy way she could converse with any adult.

"Ouch." Rich had grimaced, grabbing his chest. "I give you the alumni tour of USC, and you still shoot me down."

"Not you," Carmen had said, her tone pointed. "Just your alma mater."

How did we miss it? The subtleties of their conversation, their mannerisms.

Rich leaning over Carmen for the hot sauce, instead of asking for the bottle to be passed. Carmen shrinking back, moving away.

Were we that distracted?

"Phase two" Rich had dubbed it, gesturing with his hands as he sat at our dining table. I remembered wanting to believe the picture he was building for us, this castle in the air. But now I only see his gaze, lingering on Carmen. Hungry.

The problem I suspected she wasn't telling me, didn't want to tell me. The summer internship at Dad's company that led to her spending more time around Rich.

Those contacts Rich claimed to have at USC. Were they all just excuses for him to show up at Carmen's college volleyball matches, her dorm room?

A wave of nausea sweeps over me.

Turning on my heel, I go to the garage to get my bike and get out. Out of this house, that memory, these revelations.

The hot pavement blurs beneath my tires as I throw my weight forward, shifting gears, pedaling hard. I bike through our neighborhood with its custom homes and elaborate yards, past the stretch of soccer fields, scruffy in the midsummer heat, and cross the intersection, heading toward the duplexes where Ethan lived.

I circle his court, surprised to find myself here so quickly, so effortlessly. Like retracing a well-worn path back to that first day at the library. When I caught Ethan looking my way, the gold tints in his eyes catching the light, those perfect lips curved in a smile.

Back to a time when there was only possibility. When being together seemed as easy as drawing a line between two hearts instead of trying to bridge a galaxy of things left unsaid as we stood face to face, me stepping forward, Ethan stepping back.

One moment here, the next gone.

I swing off my bike and push it past Katheryn's old Corolla parked in the street with the yellow bumper sticker Ethan hated.

It feels strange to chain my bike to the water spigot without Ethan's bike there beside mine. To ring the doorbell instead of waiting while he fumbled in his canvas messenger bag for the house key.

"Nina." Katheryn answers the door, her voice stiff, cold, her pale blue eyes narrowed behind her rimless specs.

I open my mouth to say something. But my throat is dry, so dry, I can't make any sound at all.

Katheryn's gaze drops from my face down to my shoes and back up again.

"Come in," she says finally, taking a step back and motioning me through the door. "I'll get you a glass of water. You really shouldn't be biking in this heat."

I nod, following her from the dark hallway into the narrow kitchen. I'm suddenly aware of the sweat staining my shirt, the throbbing pain in my head, my broken, flopping shoelaces.

"Sit." Katheryn commands as she grabs a glass from the cupboard and a pitcher of filtered water from the fridge.

I slide onto one of the small wooden chairs at the kitchen table, my legs giving way, the throbbing in my head now unbearable.

"Here." She sets a full water glass in front of me.

My fingers tremble as I pick it up and lift it to my lips. I gulp quickly, water dribbling down my chin and onto the table, making a mess, as if my disheveled appearance wasn't enough.

"Slow down," Katheryn prompts, taking the chair across from me. "It's not good to drink so fast."

But I'm past caring about the way I look, the way I act.

I see only the monitor by Mr. Kishimoto's hospital bed. The numbers erased and the display reset to the program's main menu. That old wound opening as if at the turn of a key. Unlocking the pain that started it all. That first loss, its deep grief.

All those years of brushing it aside, pushing it down, like it couldn't touch me, couldn't hurt me. Ultimately pulling away from Roger, not just because of Ethan, but because of myself. Because I couldn't see Roger, couldn't be around him and not be reminded.

Of death.

But still the train whistle screams, Ethan jumps, and against the steep embankment by the railroad tracks, Carmen's body is slumped. Lips blue, no pulse.

My body shudders, tears slipping down my face and dripping into the spilled water on the table. Old tears from that first loss to the latest loss. Each wave of grief, like the turning of a page in a book. Telling the story that is, instead of the story I need it to be.

A hand touches my shoulder. I look up to find Katheryn standing beside me with a box of tissues.

"What is it, Nina?" she asks, and her voice is different, softer.

"I just—" I reach for a tissue, draw in a shaky breath. "Don't get it."

"Get what?" Katheryn asks.

"Why things would happen this way." It's hard saying this all out loud instead of in my head. Hard to have someone hear it. "I never thought—" I swallow. "That people could just—"

"Leave you?" Katheryn finishes and I nod, biting my lip.

"First, a family friend. Then Ethan, then Carmen—"

"Carmen?" Katheryn's jaw tenses. "Your sister."

I nod, lowering my gaze. "She overdosed."

Katheryn's hand tightens on my shoulder.

I fold the tissue, smaller and smaller. "By the tracks next to Ethan's cross. She's in rehab now."

"Rehab," Katheryn echoes, dropping her hand. For a second, I think she's about to say more. But she doesn't.

"Someone we knew for years, my dad's business partner, he . . . did things to her." I remember my parent's faces, frozen in disbelief, as Carmen shared her pain, her secret. Trying and failing to avoid Rich, throwing herself into school clubs, volleyball, piano, anything to distract her from what was happening. "She started using her senior year, going to people's houses, Danny's mostly, and that's where she met Ethan. And neither of them ever told me . . . anything."

In my head, I hear Mom's voice chastising me for telling things the way they are, instead of the way they should appear to be. But I'm done pretending.

"I'm sorry." Katheryn's voice is gruff. "I had it wrong. I thought you and Carmen were the ones taking Ethan deeper into his addictions."

"No." I shake my head. I only wanted to see him succeed—finish his mural, apply to art school, make the most of his limitless potential.

"He changed after starting high school," Katheryn says. "Made new friends."

I think of the rumors I had heard, of upperclassmen inviting him to parties.

"I don't know if it started with curiosity or pressure from

his peers, but I knew he was self-medicating, becoming this ... shadow of himself." Katheryn says and she looks away, her eyes red, a tear tracing her cheekbone.

On the kitchen table, her phone rings, but she makes no move to answer it.

"I tried," Katheryn says, her voice rough, raw. "I pulled him out of school junior year to do independent study, go to rehab, counseling. I even threatened to send him to Camden Military Academy, Outward Bound . . ."

"Ethan. Camping."

"Hard to picture, I guess." Katheryn's lips turn up as our eyes meet. "His dad was quite the outdoorsman. Though Ethan never knew him. As a single parent, you're only too aware of your inadequacies. Caught between the demands of working to provide and being present in their life. You want to protect them the best you can. But sometimes, you can't reach them, no matter how hard you try—"

Her voice breaks.

I thought I needed answers to all the whys. Needed to understand who Ethan was, have this all make sense to me. But it isn't a simple equation, something to solve. There are variables and complexities, things I may never understand.

So instead, I wrap my fingers around Katheryn's hand and hang on, squeezing tight. Because sometimes it's enough just to share the weight of changes and choices and pain. To lean on someone else as the world shifts beneath your feet.

Katheryn draws in a breath, squeezes back. "Would you like to see his ashes?"

In my chest, a fluttering. Hope.

"Yes," I answer, my voice shaky and imperfect. "Yes. Please."

58

PORK AND SHRIMP dumplings, chili oil dipping sauce, egg flower soup. The glass dining table immaculately set for four. Everything cooked and seasoned to perfection.

It's our first dinner with Carmen back home.

"Nina," Mom says. "The sauce, please."

I hand Mom the dish of chili oil, but her gaze is on Carmen who sits with her shoulders slumped, picking at her food. Like what's in front of her just isn't good enough.

"Do you need some sauce, Carmen?" Mom asks, her tone hopeful.

"No," Carmen snaps, shoving her plate away.

I feel my body tighten. Like nothing will ever change.

Mom's face falls. She dribbles another spoonful of sauce on her dumplings.

"So . . . what are we having tomorrow?" Carmen asks, and there's something like a challenge in her voice.

"Fish," Mom says. "With vegetables and rice."

Carmen frowns.

"Is something wrong?" Dad asks, looking up from his soup.

We glance at Carmen, tense, waiting. Still awkward around her, like she's a guest, someone new, instead of my sister, their daughter.

"I just—" Carmen draws in a breath. Exhales. "Wish we could have something else. Something that's not Chinese food."

I brace myself for Mom's response, whatever it may be. But there's only silence around the table.

"Okay," Mom says carefully. Setting down her chopsticks, she reaches for a napkin and dabs her lips. "What do you suggest?"

Carmen shifts in her seat, her hard gaze dropping as if suddenly unsure. "Maybe burgers." She shrugs. "And fries."

"I could fire up the grill," Dad offers. "Pick up a bag of frozen fries."

Mom raises her brows. "Aren't you meeting with the company accountants tomorrow to discuss the—"

"I can be home early," Dad says quickly, giving her a sharp look. "How do burgers sound for dinner tomorrow, Nina?"

It takes me a second to realize that he's asking for an opinion.

Mine.

59

IT'S 11:15 p.m. and I'm still awake, watching the shadows on my ceiling, feeling the coolness of the Delta breeze blow through my open window.

In my head, I hear Katheryn's voice. Wistful and broken as we stood in Ethan's room, his tin of ashes between us.

He's all I had. But you—you still have Carmen.

As I unlocked my bike and prepared to leave, Katheryn lingered, nodding once, before finally stepping back into that dark hall, those empty rooms. Alone, once again.

"Carmen." I tap softly on her door. "Carmen, you awake?"

A faint rustling, followed by the creak of her mattress. "Yeah," she says, her tone flat, direct. Nothing to suggest whether I'm welcome or not. "What is it?"

"I just—" I rest my hand on her doorknob. *Need you*, I want to say. But it seems like crossing a line, invisible, but understood. "I couldn't sleep," I finish instead.

"That happens."

And though the inflection in her voice doesn't change, I take that as my cue to enter, hoping for the best.

Her room is dimly lit by a single bedside lamp. Carmen sits on her cluttered bed in a plain tank top and striped pajama shorts. Her hair is loose around her shoulders and she bends over a notebook open in her lap.

"What are you doing?" I ask, stepping over the towers of books and clothes and shoes to get to her bed. In my hand, I hold the clear-view folder with Ethan's black-and-white sketch.

"Nothing."

I flinch as she claps the notebook shut, her face twisted, hard.

"I mean—" Biting her lip, Carmen looks down and away. Tries again. "I'm . . . journaling. For a support group thing."

And when she looks up, her face is more tired than twisted, a shadow of the girl in the photos tacked on the walls. The one with the confident smile and long black hair, falling perfectly in every shot.

"So, how is it?" I hedge, wondering if she's going to snap at me again. "Support group."

"Groups, actually." Carmen offers a wry smile, and there's something in it. A flicker of warmth. "Seems like there's one for every kind of issue out there."

"Even recovering musicians?"

Carmen raises her brows, and I notice her skin is smoother, more even. "You looking for a group?"

I laugh, the sound catching me by surprise. "No. Yes. Maybe."

"Why aren't you playing anymore?" Carmen gestures to a spot on her bed and I settle in beside her, placing the folder off to one side.

I wonder if she remembers how we used to pretend her bed was a lifeboat and the floor was the sea.

"There's no point, I guess." It feels easier, talking shoulder to shoulder, instead of face to face. No space between. "Especially since I'm not going to music college."

"What happened to playing just because?"

I make a face. "I don't do anything 'just because.'" No end goal, nothing to list on the resume? Why even bother?

Carmen glances down at the notebook in her lap. "We used to," she says. "All the time, with the Kishimotos."

"It was different though, back then." I counter. "There weren't any expectations."

No percentiles or statistics, college admissions articles marked up and highlighted on Mom's desk. No struggle to reach one goal, only to be presented with another, higher bar.

"Yes." Carmen's voice is forceful, bitter. "Even then, there were. So many unspoken expectations. We just didn't make them our . . . everything."

That nervous energy I felt around Mom and Grandma even as a kid. Always feeling there was something wrong with me, my faults magnified in their presence. When it was their expectations. Unspoken and oppressive.

But somehow, I didn't care as much then.

I pick at a loose thread on Carmen's comforter. "What about now?" I ask. "Are things . . . different?"

"Yes." Carmen leans back on her wrists, exhales. "And no. I mean, I know what they want for me—Mom, Dad, Grandma. It's all still there. Those expectations. But no one's pushing, forcing me to do this or that." She bites her lip. "At least when they did, I could blame them for the way things turned out. But now—"

"It's on you."

"Yeah," Carmen says, blinking quickly. "And I—" Her voice catches, one hand reaching up to touch her face. "Don't even have Ethan to talk to anymore."

"Your person," I say softly, though it still hurts to admit this. I pick up the folder and set the black-and-white sketch in Carmen's lap. "He gave that to you, not me. I can't keep it."

"I—" Carmen's voice shakes as she holds the drawing, her gaze lingering on the bottom right corner with his trademark signature. "I used to tell him everything."

My heart aches for all the times I wished I could tell Carmen everything, but couldn't. "Like what was happening with Rich."

Carmen looks away, her chin trembling.

My pain, my questions, my heaviness following Ethan's suicide. How much more did Carmen carry? Knowing him better, best.

"Did he—" I press, even though it feels hard, awkward. "Did he want you to go to the police? File a report? Get a restraining order?"

The decision we've all been waiting for Carmen to make. Hoping she'd report Rich. My parents united for once.

Carmen nods, her tears tracking down her cheeks, dripping onto her comforter. "But I *can't*, Nina." Her face crumbles as a sob racks her chest. "I just . . . *can't*."

I lean into her, wrapping my arm around her shoulders. Her body, warm and solid beside mine.

Real. Here.

"Yes," I whisper, drawing my arm tighter as she cries, her body rocking back and forth, back and forth. And it's as if there is no gap between us, in years, in looks, in worlds. "Yes, you can."

60

A ROAR. A scream. Two sets of feet pound down the stairs, through the cluttered kitchen, and out the sliding glass doors.
It's been ten months since Ethan jumped.
"Boys!" Mrs. Kishimoto chides as Roger's little brothers leapfrog over the wicker patio furniture and tumble, still screaming, onto the grass.
"Little monsters." Roger shakes his head as we take down the heavy white living room drapes, careful to fold and box them per my mom's detailed instructions.
"Better let them get it out," I say, surveying the emptiness of the room. No piano, no lamp, no charred wood coffee table. Everything gone, sold, just like that. "We won't have a yard at our new place."
"Ah, apartment life," Roger grins. The same Roger, but different at the same time. Tanner, taller, more filled out. Back from college for Thanksgiving break. "It's not as bad as you think."
"You live with *five guys*," I point out, glancing at his coarse, dark hair. He's sporting a professional cut, freshly styled with comb lines *and* product. "I'm sure it's every bit as bad as I think."
"We have standards," Roger says, defensive.

I roll my eyes. "Right."

"In fact—" Roger grabs two empty cardboard boxes from the stack in the hallway and hands me a third. "We have a cleaning schedule."

"Really." I don't even try to hide the heavy doubt in my tone.

"On a *spreadsheet*," Roger says, giving me a knowing look as we head upstairs to my room.

"Am I supposed to be impressed?"

"Very."

We pass Carmen's room, turned inside out and upside down. Dad and Carmen arguing over what to pack and what to donate.

"Too many shoes," Dad says, looking at the pile under the bed and the one by her closet doors.

"I need them all," Carmen fires back, three pairs clutched in each hand. She wears a pair of bright blue yoga pants, a large white cable-knit sweater pulled over them. There are new chestnut highlights in her short black hair. She looks nothing like the girl in the photos still tacked on her walls but everything like the one we have with us. Here, now. "For work," she clarifies. Her new job as an event coordinator.

Dad shakes his head, runs a hand through his hair, now more gray than black. "It's not going to fit, Carmen."

"We're moving into a two-bed, two-bath unit," I explain to Roger as we move down the hall to my room. "Carmen and I will be sharing a room. *If* you can imagine that."

My parents are selling the house and downgrading their cars. Mom has turned down the opportunity for another promotion. Dad is dissolving his startup and paying back what they owe. Picking up a job at the university lab in the interim.

They're cutting strings with Grandma—something they never thought possible.

"Well," Roger says, "I hear minimalism is in."

"Tell that to Carmen."

Roger laughs, his dark brown eyes finding mine. I wonder at his positivity in spite of his split with Lucy last month. Dating long distance on opposite coasts, they'd decided, was just not for them.

"So." Roger sets down the boxes and surveys my room. "What are we packing?"

"Everything in the closet is going," I answer. "But I still need to sort through the things in my desk and dresser."

From downstairs, I hear the heavy clang of the oven door, the beep of the timer being set. Mom and Mrs. Kishimoto chattering as they pack up the kitchen, like there's not enough time in the world for all the things they want to say.

"Your Mom mentioned you're taking some community college classes," Roger says, pulling my sheet music binders and tubs of summer clothes down from the shelves in my closet. I can't help but notice his shoulders. They're broader, more muscular, his San Diego State T-shirt fitting just right. "How's that going?"

"Just some general ed. classes. Things I can transfer, once I figure out what's next."

"And music?"

"What about it?"

"You know," Roger says, undeterred, "your passion?"

I shrug, brushing it off. But he's handing me my old violin case, the one I keep on the top shelf in my closet.

"Come on, Nina." Roger smiles, just the way I remember. "Play something."

I shake my head. "This isn't even tuned. It's too small—"

"Excuses, excuses." Roger tsks, moving closer, his presence solid, familiar, safe. "Just a little ditty, for old times' sake. Something original."

"Ditty?" I repeat, undoing the clasps and opening the case, acutely aware of his nearness. "That's not even a—"

I stare down at the black T-shirt, neatly folded on top of my old violin. DAVIS HIGH SCHOOL ORCHESTRA in light blue lettering framed by white baby wings, flying music notes, a bald eagle soaring into a sunset. Ethan's gift to me.

I wait for that familiar pressure in my chest, that old ache. But instead, I smell Mrs. Kishimoto's snickerdoodles wafting from the kitchen downstairs. Filling my senses, that space, with something sweet and warm and good.

Like other recent victories—passing my driver's test, having lunch with Katheryn, standing beside Carmen as she filed restraining order papers and a police report against Rich Bashir.

I rosin my bow and tune my violin. Fingers fumbling as I tighten a peg here, loosen a peg there. Falling, falling, into Roger's smile.

Taking a breath, I draw my bow across the strings. Listening.

For a single, rising note.

Acknowledgments

SPECIAL THANKS TO those who make this book possible: Kris Ann Valdez for creating connections. My agent, Erica Martin, for championing my writing and this book. Soho Press Senior Editor, Alexa Wejko, for your unparalleled vision, guidance, and boundless enthusiasm (!!!). The amazing Soho team—Managing Editor, Rachel Kowal; Art and Production Director, Janine Agro; and Senior Publicist, Erica Loberg—for tirelessly producing and promoting this book. The incorrigible Pen-in-Hand writers group which has been there every step of the way. Go-to draft readers, Sarah Aher and Pauly Heller. My dad, for fostering in me a deep love of stories. My mom, for always encouraging and believing in me. Partner-in-crime, Adam Parker, for your unwavering support and insight. *Thank you.*